THE ISLE OF SONG

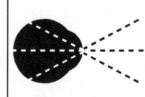

THE ISLE OF SONG

HILARY WILDE

THORNDIKE PRESS

An imprint of Thomson Gale, a part of The Thomson Corporation

THOMSON
GALE

Detroit • New York • San Francisco • New Haven, Conn. • Waterville, Maine • London

THOMSON
━━━━━✦━━━━━ ™
GALE

LIBRARY OF CONGRESS CATALOGING-IN-PUBLICATION DATA

Wilde, Hilary.
  The isle of song / by Hilary Wilde.
    p. cm. — (Thorndike Press large print Candlelight)
  ISBN-13: 978-1-4104-0272-1 (alk. paper)
  ISBN-10: 1-4104-0272-X (alk. paper)
  1. Large type books. I. Title.
PR6072.E735I85 2007
823'.914—dc22   2007032083

Published in 2007 by arrangement with Juliet Burton Literary Agency.

Printed in the United States of America on permanent paper
10 9 8 7 6 5 4 3 2 1

THE ISLE OF SONG

CHAPTER ONE

Kate swayed as she stood. There was a smell of wet mackintoshes and she had to cling to the strap above her as the train hurtled its way towards Ealing. She could see over the shoulder of a short man in front of her, and the photograph on the page of the newspaper he was holding seemed to rush up to meet her.

Simon Ellison.

She knew the face well, for he was always in the news. A wealthy stockbroker with a promising future, everyone said. She wondered what he was really like. Only that day at the solicitor's office where Kate worked as book-keeper, she had heard them discussing him. The general impression she had gathered was that he was a hard and ruthless man.

Looking at his photograph, she wondered. He was in his early thirties and had a lean humorous face that ended surprisingly in a square stubborn chin. Although his hair was short and blond, he had thick dark eyebrows and his eyes, while amused, yet held a wary look.

Swaying with the train, she had some difficulty in reading the smaller print under his name, but it said that recently Simon Ellison had inherited an island in the South Pacific from an eccentric great-aunt and had, while visiting it, nearly been killed in a violent cyclone. Now, the article went on to say, speculation was rife as to what he planned to do with the island. Would he sell it? It had tremendous potentialities as a playground for wealthy tourists as it was not far from Tahiti and the lovely town of Papeete, known generally as the Paris of the Pacific.

At last the train reached Ealing and Kate rushed to queue for the bus, holding her emerald green umbrella up against the pelting rain, but her shoulder-length honey-brown hair, that swung as she ran, was soon wet. A short bus ride, a quick run down the quiet suburban road and she was home. Even as she fumbled for the key, the front door swung open as if they were waiting for her. Tired as she was, for several of the staff were sick and Kate had tangled with a lot of work all day, she knew dismay.

What was wrong? Why were they waiting for her so impatiently? And then she smelt the fragrant odour of fried onions and chops and knew her first premonition was right. Something was definitely wrong — otherwise why would Nancy have bothered to cook the dinner?

Kate was nearly twenty years old and for the past four years had kept house for her brother, sister and stepfather. She had grown used to the mad rush that was her everyday life; flying round after cooking breakfast while she made beds and straightened rooms, then rushing home at night to cook the dinner. Mike was only nine years old and Nancy just seventeen, so they were not much help. This was the first time in months that they had bothered to cook the meal for her. Why tonight?

She gazed down at Mike's pale little face and saw how clean it was and that his fair hair was smoothed down with water. His eyes were shining brightly as he gazed at her, and then when Nancy came running as well, Kate's heart sank even more. Nancy's honey-gold hair was brushed up into a knot on top of her head, she was wearing one of her prettiest blue shifts, and her face was as radiant as Mike's.

Something had happened, Kate knew.

There was something the family wanted her to agree to. They knew that she couldn't and so were ganging up on her, planning to soften her. Then as Nancy kissed her warmly, Kate felt ashamed, but unfortunately she had grown cynical of recent years, and when her stepfather, Jerome, joined them in the hall, she knew her first premonition was right. Something was up!

Jerome was a wisp of a man with receding greyish hair and — as Kate's mother had often said in the years gone by — the appetite of a horse, the shape of a greyhound, the eyes of a dreamer and the mouth of a poet. Jerome was a darling but a very bad provider. He admitted it himself. He had restless feet and was always searching for perfection and being disappointed, only to bounce up again to start looking once more.

'My poor Kate,' Jerome said, his voice affectionate. 'You look like a drowned rat.'

'We lit the fire,' Nancy said eagerly. 'And the dinner's ready.'

Kate tried to smile, but her tiredness swept over her. Trouble lay ahead, and she wondered how she would have strength enough to meet it. Jerome's excited face gave her a hint of what was coming and her tired unhappy mind swerved away violently from the thought. If it was that, she could not bear it . . .

They ate in a state of suppressed excitement. Mike kept opening his mouth eagerly, glancing at Nancy, and closing it shut quickly, but his eyes went on shining. Nancy and Jerome kept exchanging significant glances, and Kate felt that she was all alone, with the three of them against her.

She stifled a sigh. She was so tired of always being the one to make decisions, to keep them in line with their narrow budget, to see that the bills were paid up to date, that Mike's shoes were repaired and that he and Nancy went regularly to the dentist. Everything was such a fight, and she was tired of being father and mother, for Jerome was a dreamer and seemed completely unaware of the material things of life.

There was a sudden silence that filled Kate with uneasiness. She tried to think of something to say to postpone what was coming, but then Mike spoke. It was as if the words bubbled out beyond his control.

'Daddy's got a job on a South Sea island!' he said excitedly.

Kate stared at him. So it was what she had feared!

'Oh no!' she exclaimed, her voice laced with the dismay she could not hide. Jerome could not do this to her! How could she manage to meet the weekly instalments on the house? Feed and clothe them all and cope with Nancy's bursts of extravagance?

The saddest part of Jerome's marriage to Kate's mother had been the long years he was overseas, always looking for the ideal job and never finding it; coming home for exciting leaves and going off again. Vividly Kate could recall how she had clung to him after her mother's death, weeping in his arms, begging him not to leave them. She had been sixteen and terrified of how she'd manage. Was she any more capable of looking after them alone, now?

'And we're all going with him, Kate,' Nancy said, her voice shrill, her three-cornered face aglow with excitement, her eyes bright.

Kate turned to look at her stepfather and saw the anxiety in his eyes, saw, too, the nervous way he was jiggling with a fork on the table. A terrible thought hit her. Jerome was scared of her.

It seemed so absurd that she wanted to laugh and cry at the same time, and then she knew that it was not absurd. He was afraid she would rub out yet another of his dreams. Yet it was ridiculous to think they could all pack up and go off to the South Pacific. How could they?

Jerome stood up. 'Nancy — Mike, clear away and wash up. Kate's tired. Come into my den with me, Kate. I should have broken it more gently. I'll tell you everything.'

She felt dazed as he led the way, holding her arm gently. Jerome's den was — unlike his bedroom — a model of tidiness. A trestle table dominated the room so that there was barely space to walk round it, and on it were spread out new clean sheets of paper on which he had already started drawing.

Jerome gently pushed her into the one chair, a dilapidated rocking chair that had been in their family for several generations.

'Just relax, Kate. I won't take the job if you disapprove,' Jerome said gently. 'Close your eyes for a moment. You're tired.'

Kate obeyed. The tears smarted behind her closed lids. Again the onus was on her. If she disapproved . . . Why must she always be the one to give the veto to the things they wanted to do?

In a moment, Jerome was back, pushing a glass in her hand. She looked at him.

He smiled, his thin face lighting up. 'I know you don't drink normally, Kate darling, but you need this. It's very weak.'

The whisky warmed and stung her throat, but it did seem to untie the knot she was in. As she looked at him, where he sat perched on an upturned wastepaper basket, she managed to smile.

'Tell me, Jerome. I'll try to understand.'

He leaned forward, clasping his hands tightly, obviously keeping his voice under control.

'It happened suddenly, Kate. Today when I was working, the general manager sent for me and introduced me to this man. He inherited an island in the South Seas.'

'Not Simon Ellison?' Kate asked in dismay.

'You know him?' Jerome asked quickly.

Kate shook her head. 'Only of him, Jerome. They were talking about him in the office. Saying he drove a hard bargain — that he was ruthless and mercenary . . .'

Jerome looked shocked. 'They're quite wrong. I admit he wants his pound of flesh, but he's prepared to pay for it. I liked him.'

Kate half-smiled. Jerome liked everyone; that was one of his endearing and most exasperating characteristics.

'Sorry I interrupted you, Jerome. You were saying . . . ?'

'Where was I? Oh yes, Simon Ellison told me he had inherited this island and flew out to see it. It's a wonderful place, classic South Sea islands stuff. Unspoilt, incredibly beautiful. His great-aunt, whom he did not know — for it seems she was the black sheep of the family — had lived there in solitary but extravagant style. He was only there a few days when this terrific cyclone hit the place. Many of the buildings have been completely destroyed. He says it was tragic. Anyhow now he intends to turn it into a tourist resort —'

'And make a fortune.'

Jerome looked startled. 'Of course he might at that, but I don't think that's his aim.'

'You wouldn't,' Kate said with a quick smile. 'You're an idealist, Jerome. You think the best of everyone.'

Jerome looked at her worriedly. 'And you're beginning to think the worst. My poor Kate, what are we doing to you?'

Kate found to her dismay that his tender voice had brought tears to her eyes. 'Nothing,' she said hoarsely. 'It's the way I'm made.'

Jerome jumped to his feet. 'The car will be here in a moment. Do you want to do your face?'

'The car?' Kate was startled.

Jerome nodded. 'Simon Ellison wants to meet you and is sending his car for us.'

'But why?' Kate was on her feet, her face dismayed.

'I explained to him I had a family and couldn't just walk out,' Jerome told her. 'I said I'd promised to stay with you all — and quite right, too. My place is with you. That was when he suggested you all came with me and . . . and I said I didn't think you'd . . .' Jerome hesitated. 'You're such a practical, down-to-earth person, Kate, I just couldn't see that you would accept the idea. I know it sounds crazy, but . . .'

'Mr. Ellison thinks he can convert me?' Kate said coldly.

Jerome caught her arm. 'Kate,' he said earnestly, 'we won't go if you don't want to, but at least hear what Mr. Ellison has to say. Won't you?'

Kate took a long deep breath. The onus was on her. Always on her. If she agreed that they could go and it was all a terrible flop, it would be her fault. If she fought them over this and kept them here in England, they would never forget or forgive her for depriving them of the chance to see the world.

'Of course,' Kate said. 'I'll just run and do my face. I must look a sight.'

Jerome smiled at her. 'You always look lovely to me,' he said simply.

Kate fled upstairs to the bedroom she shared with Nancy. She stood in the middle of the room, her hands pushed against her mouth. How badly Nancy wanted to go — just look at the spotlessly tidy room. Nancy had even turned down Kate's bed for the night and put her pyjamas ready.

Kate went to the mirror and stared at herself. Was she such an ogre? Had they to crawl — to beseech her to agree to something they all wanted?

'Kate, the car's here,' Jerome shouted.

'C-coming!' she called back.

She leaned close to the mirror and applied powder and some lipstick. She had such an ordinary face — golden-brown eyes — a rather large mouth — a thin nose. No beauty there. What would Simon Ellison think of her? Or would he even see her? Wouldn't she merely be an obstacle to something he wanted that had to be removed?

Quickly she ran a brush down her shoulder-length bob of honey-brown hair. It was straight as a die, but by wearing it this way, she could set it herself and save a lot of money.

An enormous car was waiting for them — a shining black Rolls-Royce. Nancy's eyes were wide with awe as she watched Kate hurry through the rain under the enormous umbrella the uniformed chauffeur held over them. Mike was standing close to Nancy, and as he waved goodbye to Kate, Kate saw that he had his fingers crossed.

Somehow that hurt more than anything else. They all wanted this incredibly daft adventure, and if she denied them it . . . yet if she agreed and they lost everything they had slowly and painfully built up.

'What about the house, Jerome?' she said.

He turned to her eagerly as the car moved forward.

'We could let it. I can put it in the hands of the agents and they'd pay the instalments and anything over would be saved for repairs.'

'And Mike's schooling . . .'

'There's a school on the island.'

'My job, Jerome? I'm due for a rise next year, and Nancy's doing so well with the advertising firm and . . .'

Jerome's hand closed over hers reassuringly. 'Stop worrying, Kate. Simon Ellison says he'll have work enough for you both on the island and will pay you good wages which, as we shall live board free, you can save. Besides . . .' He hesitated a moment. 'You and Nancy lead such narrow lives here, Kate. Never getting the chance to see the world or meeting . . .'

Kate found herself laughing. 'Wealthy

husbands? I can hear Nancy talking!' She felt a warm rush of affection for her stepfather. It was not his fault he was a dreamer, for he was the kindest man in the world.

How well she could remember when her own father had died. She had been very young and Nancy little more than a baby. There had been difficult lonely years while her mother battled to rear them alone, and then she had met Jerome and home had become a warm place again, even though he was away from it so much, for there were always his letters to await and his long leaves, and then Mike had been born, and they had seemed like a real family.

Jerome held her hand tightly. 'Just wait until you've talked to Mr. Ellison, Kate.'

Kate smiled wryly as she turned her head away. Obviously Simon Ellison had made it plain to Jerome that he could handle her! He had that sort of face — arrogant, a little patronizing. Why did it mean so much to him to have Jerome work for him? It was true Jerome was a good architect, but many people thought his ideas too fantastic to become realities.

The car drew up outside a big grey building in a quiet square. The silent solicitous chauffeur escorted them across the wet pavement, trying to shelter them from the rain, but Kate's feet and legs were soon wet as the rain splashed up from the pavement. The front door opened and a butler, portly and impressive, led them across a lofty hall with a tiled floor. He opened a door, announced them and stood to one side.

Kate's first glimpse was one of incredible luxury. The deep pile of the dark blue carpet, the gold furniture with gold silk brocade cushions, the oil paintings on the walls, great splurges of violent colour — and then she saw the man.

She recognized him instantly. And yet he looked quite different from the photographs she had seen. Younger and much better looking.

He seemed to unfold from a chair and stood before them — one of the tallest men she had ever seen, thin with a hard wiry strength that was impressive as she came forward with long effortless strides.

'Ah — Jerome. Good,' he said.

He had a deep voice, warm, friendly. His eyebrows were black tufts just as in his photograph, and they emphasized the curious look in his eyes as he turned to Kate.

'Is this your eldest stepdaughter?' he said, his voice sceptical.

Jerome smiled. 'Yes, this is Kate. She's nearly twenty. Kate, this is Mr. Ellison.'

Kate smiled stiffly, holding her body tensely as she looked up at the man who was looking her over with a rather supercilious smile.

He held her hand for a moment. His hand was cold.

'Thank you for coming along,' he said. His voice was as cold as his hand had been. He turned to Jerome. 'I wonder if you'd mind going into the library.' He pointed to a door leading out of the room. 'I've got some photographs there I'd like your opinion of. If you're coming with me, we haven't got too much time to spare.'

'Of course,' Jerome said with a smile. He looked at Kate — for a moment she thought he was going to say something and then he merely smiled at her and walked away.

Simon Ellison was scrupulously polite, seating Kate in a comfortable chair, putting a small glass of sherry by her side, offering her a cigarette which she refused.

And then he straddled a chair opposite her, resting his hands on the back of it and looking at her.

'You're certainly different from what I expected,' he said.

She felt colour in her checks. 'And you're exactly what I expected,' she said sharply.

He lifted his eyebrows. 'I see you've heard of me.'

'Who hasn't? You're always in the papers, and . . .' She stopped. She had not meant to sound so rude, but something about him irritated her. Why was he looking at her in that patronizing manner? Why that drily amused smile? Was she being naïve?

'Of course. I splashed the headlines in the paper today, didn't I?' He chuckled. 'Well, what was your first reaction to this idea?'

'I was shocked,' Kate said bluntly.

He nodded. 'Jerome reckoned you'd be. He'd have jumped at the chance, but he said he had his family to consider. A family can be a millstone round a man's neck.'

'A man shouldn't have a family if he's going to see them as a millstone,' Kate said sharply.

'*Touché!*' Simon Ellison agreed. 'Tell me, what have you against the idea? Most girls would jump at the chance of a few years in the South Pacific Islands.'

'Few years?' Kate said, horrified. 'What about Mike's schooling?'

'How old is he? Yes, I remember, nearly ten. Right? Jerome told me. Well, we have a small but adequate school on the island. If you distrust that, you can get correspondence lessons sent out. Look, Miss Bayliss

— suppose you give me a rough idea of your reasons for your hesitation about this. I can assure you your step-father will get an excellent salary, and I'm offering you all free board and accommodation. In addition, if you and your sister want work, I am prepared to pay for your services. You must admit it's a generous offer and . . .'

'Generous? Too generous,' Kate said. 'We don't want charity.'

The red flames of anger were in her cheeks again.

Simon Ellison looked startled. 'It was not intended as charity, Miss Bayliss. Your stepfather is a talented man and I'm prepared to pay highly for his services.' He leaned forward. 'I think I understand. You have no faith in him, have you?'

Kate swallowed nervously. 'I — of course I have, but . . .'

'He's been a bad provider, hasn't he? He feels this very keenly. And you are the one who's responsible for his feeling guilty.' Simon Ellison's voice was suddenly stern and unfriendly. 'Don't you know that the most brutal thing you can do to any man is to show him you have no faith in him?'

'It's not fair to say that,' Kate said quickly. 'You don't know what it's like to be sixteen or seventeen and have to beg the grocer for an extension of credit that has already been extended beyond . . . beyond . . .' She bit her lips, afraid because her voice had begun to tremble. Simon Ellison was the sort of man who would accuse her of using tears as a weapon. 'You can't possibly know what it's like to be afraid you'll be evicted for not keeping up payments on the house — not being able to buy the right kind of food . . . Jerome has been in and out of jobs and . . .'

'Because he's an unhappy disillusioned man with a great talent that has never been used. Why have you kept him tied to you — why didn't you let him go overseas and find the jobs he can do well? He'd have sent you money regularly.'

'Oh yes, I know,' Kate said bitterly. 'I remember when my mother was alive. How we'd wait for those regular cheques that came so irregularly. There was always a good reason for the delay — we knew it was never Jerome's fault. He wouldn't hurt us if he could help it, but there was always something. Then the change in currency wasn't always on our side. Mother had to go out to work and . . . and I was only sixteen when she died. I got a job right away as an office girl, but I was going to be a teacher and . . .'

'There wasn't money enough for it?'

'There wasn't money, period,' Kate said

bitterly. 'I got the first job I could and studied book-keeping and typing at night. I got a neighbour — I had to pay her — to feed Nancy and Mike when they came home from school. Even so, I had to have Jerome there with his regular salary — we couldn't have managed. After all, he is Mike's father and . . .'

Simon Ellison went on staring at her thoughtfully, and suddenly she disliked him more than she had ever disliked any man before.

'It's so easy for you,' she said angrily. 'You're wealthy and secure. But we — we had nothing. What would you have done in my place?'

He looked at her thoughtfully. 'Probably the same thing, Miss Bayliss — but I hope not.' He drained his glass and went to refill it.

She sat very still. What was that he had said? 'But I hope not.' Had she been wrong in asking Jerome for help? Did Simon Ellison think she should have managed on her own? Was he mad? Or just plain selfishly stupid?

He came back and sat down again. 'You don't drink sherry?'

'Sometimes.' She sipped the sherry slowly. It wasn't fair. She was always the one to be blamed for everything.

'And this job, Miss Bayliss,' Simon Ellison said, his voice cool. 'You don't think Jerome should accept it?'

Kate swallowed. 'I don't know enough about it to judge, Mr. Ellison. In any case, the decision is Jerome's.'

'He said the decision is yours.'

'But that's not . . .' she began, but stopped. Whatever happened he must not see how hurt she was. She lifted her head and looked at him. 'What does the job entail, Mr. Ellison? How many years? What sort of climate would there be? Mike is delicate and used to get asthma badly. Nancy is seventeen — would there be anyone of her age there?'

'The contract would be for three years, but if at any time during that period any of you, apart from your stepfather, of course, wished to leave the island, I would arrange to pay your fares back to England,' Simon said stiffly. 'My great-aunt had a commodious residence and there would be room for us all to live there without intruding on one another's privacy. The climate is temperate and healthy — there's a resident doctor and a hospital. There is also, as I told you, a small but adequate school. If you and your sister care to work for me, I'm prepared to pay you —'

When he named a figure, Kate gasped.

'All that and free board and lodging? It doesn't make sense!'

He smiled. It was the first time, she realized, that he had smiled at her.

'But it does make sense to me, Miss Bayliss,' he said. 'Your stepfather is the architect I've been looking for — a dreamer and a poet who yet is capable of turning his dreams and fantasies into facts. I don't want a conventional architect or one who refuses to listen to my own ideas. I've talked to your stepfather and I like his views on modern architecture. I feel that we could work well together. I always find that a happy employee is a good loyal worker, and if it will make Jerome happy to have his family with him, I'm prepared to accept you.'

'In other words we are on . . . on sufferance.'

'That rather depends on you, Miss Bayliss. Sufferance is a strange word. Let's say that I hope we can become a happy community, each one contributing something to the general effort.'

'What are your plans for the island?'

'I intend to make it into a tourist centre. To continue, you asked about young people. My accountant, Adam, is in his mid-twenties, and my nephew, who is not yet twenty, will probably be with us also. In addition, doubtless there will be other young people as our plans progress and more staff are required. You need not fear loneliness . . .' He paused and frowned. 'I forgot one thing, Miss Bayliss. Neither you nor your sister are engaged to be married?'

She felt herself stiffen. 'Neither of us.'

He gave her a strange searching look. 'I don't mean to be rude, Miss Bayliss, but I'm rather surprised. An attractive girl like yourself . . . but then maybe you don't believe in love?' His voice was amused, and she fidgeted in her chair as she felt her cheeks grow hot.

'I do believe in love, Mr. Ellison,' she said as formally as she could. 'But so far there just hasn't been much time.'

'Of course not.' His eyes were amused. They were strange eyes, a mixture of grey and gold, and he had long dark lashes that threw shadows on his cheeks. Now he opened his eyes wide as he looked at her, even more searchingly. 'I forgot you are the mainstay of your family. Naturally there's been no time for pleasure.'

Kate bit her lip angrily. 'I haven't met anyone I wanted to . . .' she began.

He nodded. 'Very wise. Best to walk warily and not rush in, Miss Bayliss. Personally, I feel this wonderful love that sentimental songs and romantic novels are full of just doesn't exist. It's become too commercialized to have any real value today. As you say, you want to be very, very sure. I've seen so much misery as a result of this so-called wonderful love that I steer very clear of it. Very clear indeed.' There was a strongly emphasized significance in his voice, and she wondered if he meant her to take it as a warning.

A warning? Of what? Warning her not to look at him romantically? She wanted to laugh. He was the last man in the world she would look at like that.

He stood up. 'I'm sure you're tired, Miss Bayliss, after your long day. I suggest you think over my offer and let me know in the morning.' His voice was curt and unfriendly.

Kate stood up. It annoyed her to have to look up at him. He must be well over six foot tall, for she was not a short girl. Her hair swung with the movement and she wondered why he stared at her so oddly. Was her nose shining?

It was in that moment that she made up her mind.

'I don't need to think over the offer, Mr. Ellison. The decision is my stepfather's, and as he obviously wants to accept your offer, I wouldn't attempt to stop him. Your terms are most generous —' She deliberately kept her voice cold and unfriendly in turn. Whatever happened, he must be made to know that she had no interest in him whatsoever. 'And I think we'd be foolish to refuse such an offer. I know both Mike and Nancy are very excited at this opportunity to see something of the world, and . . .'

'You are not?' he said curtly.

She lifted her head and looked at him. 'On the contrary, Mr. Ellison,' she said, 'I've always wanted to see the South Sea Islands.'

'Good.' He half-turned away, then looked back. 'If you care to sit down and finish your sherry, I'll tell Jerome the good news.'

She sat down and finished the sherry. Why did she dislike him so much? Was it his patronizing attitude? The way he looked at her? His rudeness — for he had been rude. Implying she ruled the household and wore the trousers, that she had been unfair to Jerome . . .

When Jerome came from the library with Simon Ellison and she saw the incredulous happiness on Jerome's face, Kate drew a long deep breath. Had he really been so sure she would refuse to let him go? Had she really that much power over him? It was a terrible thought. How had it happened? Did he see them all as a millstone round his neck? As Simon Ellison obviously saw them.

Jerome came straight to her. 'Oh, Kate, my dear girl, how glad I am you think it's a good idea.'

'I . . .' she began stiffly, and over Jerome's shoulders, she met Simon Ellison's stern gaze. 'I think it's a wonderful idea, Jerome,' she said instead.

Jerome looked round at Simon. 'I'll speak to the general manager tomorrow, Mr. Ellison. I'm sure he'll release me.'

'Good. I want you to get stuck into that research right away.' Simon turned to Kate. 'Can you give a week's notice? You'll have a lot to do, getting packed and the house ready for letting, but my secretary will be glad to help you.' He smiled coldly. 'We leave in two weeks' time.'

'Two weeks?' Kate gasped. 'But our passports, our inoculations . . .'

'My secretary will arrange everything,' Simon said curtly. He gave Kate a card. 'Ring her tomorrow and she'll tell you what to do. I'll see you on the plane. By the way . . .' his voice changed as he looked at Jerome, 'just skip the Mister, please, Jerome. My name's Simon.'

Jerome glowed. 'Of course, Mr. — I mean, Simon. I just can't wait to get to work on those suggestions of yours.'

'Would you like to take those papers home tonight and browse through them?' Simon asked him. 'They're on the table in the library.'

The instant Jerome had left them, Simon turned to the silent Kate. 'Well, Kate,' he said, 'I want to make a bet with you.'

'A bet?' she echoed, startled.

He was smiling at her, but the smile did not reach his eyes. 'Yes, a bet. Just that if in six months' time, you don't admit that this was a good idea not only for Jerome but for the lot of you, then I'll give a thousand pounds to your favourite charity.'

She stared at him in amazement. 'A thousand pounds? But . . .'

'I can't lose,' he said, still smiling.

'And if . . .'

'If you are happy and it was a good idea? Well, you'll have to pay a forfeit. I'll think up something in the months ahead.'

Jerome joined them, his arms full of papers. 'We'd better be going,' he said.

Simon saw them to the door. The chauffeur was waiting, the umbrella at the ready. The rain was still teeming down, the roads awash with water.

'Kate, I don't know how to thank you,'

Jerome said, his voice thick as they got into the car.

'Don't try,' Kate said crisply. 'It's a good job, good pay and the chance of a holiday for us. We'd be fools to turn it down.'

'I was so afraid you'd . . .'

'Jerome, please!' Kate turned to him desperately. 'You make me sound like an ogre or a tyrant or something. It was just that I couldn't manage on my own. Jerome, I was so young then, and scared and . . .'

His arm went round her as he pulled her close. 'Why, Kate darling, I never thought or suggested you were an ogre. My place was with you. Even if you hadn't asked me to stay with you, I couldn't have left you. But this is a wonderful chance, and something big might come of it. Simon will be a good man to work for and I should get some excellent publicity. Best of all, we'll all be together, and it will be a wonderful unusual new way of living. You'll love it, Kate. What made you finally agree? Did Simon talk you into it?'

Kate bit her lip quickly, stopping the words she wanted to say. 'Of course not,' she said instead, and told the truth. 'When I realized that you all wanted it so badly . . .'

'We do, Kate. It's a dream come true. A South Pacific Island . . . Simon's a nice chap, isn't he?'

'Nice?' Kate began. She was about to say sarcastically that she found Simon the most rude, objectionable, selfish, impossible man she had ever met, but fortunately the car chose that moment to stop and she realized they were home and the chauffeur opening the door for them.

The front door of their house flew open even before they had left the car and Mike and Nancy came racing through the rain to meet them.

'Is it all right?' they shouted in excited unison.

'Daddy, Daddy!' Mike added shrilly. 'Is it all right?'

'Yes, it's all right,' Jerome said, his voice husky. 'Everything's all right, darlings.'

CHAPTER TWO

It was a wet spring morning when they walked across the tarmac towards the huge plane. Mike was clinging to Kate's hand, giving a skip of excitement every few moments, his usually pale cheeks flushed with excitement. Nancy seemed to be walking on air, her eyes shining brightly. Kate noticed that every now and then Jerome gave Kate a little anxious look, so she smiled often and talked gaily to Miss Stern, Simon Ellison's middle-aged secretary, who had been such a tower of strength during the hectic fortnight that had just passed.

'You're going to love every moment of it,' Miss Stern said, her spectacles swinging from a gold chain round her neck, her mauve-blue hair piled high under a smart hat, her yellow umbrella dipping as she moved jerkily on her high-heeled shoes.

'I'm sure,' Kate said brightly.

Miss Stern had brought them records of

haunting, lovely music so that the small house in Ealing had resounded with Pacific melodies, books about Tahiti, and Nancy and Kate had read them avidly, talking of the deep-sea fishing they planned to do — while Kate shuddered silently at the thought of sharks — and the wonders of the dancing they would see and the mountains and tropical flowers.

What a mad rush the two weeks had been. Without Miss Stern's able management, Kate knew they could never have been ready. A tenant to find for the house, everything packed in storage save for what they were taking. Jerome's handsome advance cheque to be spent on clothes bought under Miss Stern's tuition and finally Miss Stern's friendly little words of advice to Kate.

'The mosquitoes are the serpents in this Eden,' she had said, putting a cigarette carefully into her long jade-green holder. 'You must always sleep under mosquito nets, Kate. That's terribly important. Oh yes, you must always wear sneakers on the beach or your feet'll get cut on the coral. January and December are the cyclone months, so you'll be all right until then. You're going at the best time, for the season is temperate just now and you'll have trade winds to cool things down.'

'I wish you were coming with us,' Kate said impulsively.

Miss Stern's eyes twinkled. 'If I were your age, nothing would stop me, but I've my own little flat in Bayswater and my car and friends. You'll love it, I know.'

Would she? Kate wondered rather miserably as they walked towards the huge plane. Maybe it was pure cussedness on her part, but the more excited the rest of the family grew, the more uncertain she felt.

How long would Nancy's enthusiasm last? She was a moody girl and easily got depressed. Suppose Nancy wanted to come back to England? Simon Ellison would pay her return fare, but could Kate let Nancy, at seventeen years of age, come back alone? And if Kate came back with Nancy, could she leave Mike alone with his father?

Kate realized suddenly how desperately tired she was. There had been so much to do — photographs to be taken, vaccination and various injections which Miss Stern had advised. Then Kate got in touch with a correspondence school for Mike's education, just in case the school on the island was not as good as Simon Ellison had implied.

At the gangway, they bade Miss Stern farewell.

She kissed Kate warmly. 'Don't worry about a thing, dear. Everything's under control. You'll be met in Paris and Mr. Ellison will be waiting in Los Angeles for you. Now, you have got those travel pills?'

Kate nodded. 'Mike and I have taken some.'

'Good. Then happy flying!'

Despite her weariness, Kate felt excited as they boarded the plane amidst a buzz of laughter and voices and the trim, pretty little air hostess settled them in their seats. Then came the warming-up of the engines, the slow trundling into position, the curt announcement about safety belts as Kate helped Mike with his and did up her own.

Mike's hand held Kate's tightly as the expected moment came and the plane gathered speed down the runway, and then suddenly, almost before they realized it, they had left the wet grey April weather behind them and were up above the woolly-looking clouds in brilliant sunshine and staring at the incredibly blue sky.

'The most exciting moment of my life,' Mike said solemnly.

Kate smiled at him, resisting the desire to give him a big hug. Well, whatever happened, at least Mike would never forget this moment. Even if the whole project — as

Mike called it — flopped, they would have seen something of the world.

She leaned back in her seat and relaxed, closing her eyes, thinking of the past two weeks with the rushing around and the excitement that had flooded the small house in Ealing.

Almost at once, Mike was nudging her excitedly to point out the white cliffs of Dover so far below. The plane was still climbing fast. When would they see England again? Kate wondered, with a quick moment of fear. Should they have stayed where they were? Would Mike be all right in a sultry tropical country?

Suddenly they were over France and approaching Paris. The whole journey had taken an hour!

Paris! One of Simon Ellison's staff met them — tall, handsome and with a French gallantry that obviously delighted Nancy. As they sat in the restaurant having coffee, Kate realized that streaks and spots were dancing in front of her eyes. She knew a moment of panic. She had not had a migraine for years. She couldn't be having one now! The flow of laughter and shrill voices in many languages seemed to be hitting against her mind like ruthless bullets. She closed her eyes, fighting the faint nausea. When no one was looking she swallowed three more of the tablets Miss Stern had advised her to buy.

The rest of the trip was a nightmare with only moments of consciousness for Kate. No sooner had the plane taken off than Kate had to rush to the washroom, meeting the dismayed but sympathetic eyes of the air hostess as she passed her — and then everything went black and a man was bending over her, his hazy face sympathetic.

'I'm a doctor. Migraine, eh?' he asked.

Vaguely Kate felt herself helped back to her feet, given a glass of water and some pills to swallow. As though from far away, she heard Nancy saying crossly:

'Now why has she to be sick at this time?'

And loyal Mike's angry reply. 'Oh, shut up, Nancy, you don't think she likes being ill, do you?'

And then Jerome's anxious sympathetic voice. 'You should have told us, darling, we could have stayed in Paris.'

Kate closed her eyes tightly. And been a nuisance to them and caused trouble to Simon Ellison? That was the last thing she would do.

It was a terrible five hours as she prayed silently for the plane to land so that she might crawl into a dark hole, away from bright lights, noise of laughter and voices, the vibration that seemed to intensify her nausea. At last the plane touched ground. Jerome helped her, for she was absurdly shaky.

'Los Angeles!' Nancy was saying, her voice awed.

Kate put her hand to her eyes quickly as the sunshine blinded her. A stout man was by their side, introducing himself as Erasmus Shay, saying Mr. Ellison was detained but would join them soon. Mr. Shay found a chair for Kate while he sped them through Customs and the necessary formalities. Kate was in a daze most of the time, trying to smile and speak, her head aching, the strange shapes before her eyes obscuring her vision. But she saw that the car waiting for them was cream and luxurious and the hotel when they reached it was the tallest building she had ever seen. Mike's excited comments and Nancy's eager voice as she bombarded Mr. Shay with questions only added to Kate's misery, and it was a relief to be in the hotel bedroom, shedding her clothes, crawling into bed after she had drawn the curtains.

Jerome came and hovered anxiously. 'A doctor . . .'

'No, please, Jerome,' Kate begged. 'Just let

me sleep it off.'

She dozed, and awoke to the sound of Simon Ellison's deep voice. Reluctantly Kate opened her eyes, and it seemed like the proverbial last straw. She wanted to turn her face to the wall and cry. Why must he see her looking like this — shiny nose, reddened eyes, ghastly colour in her cheeks?

Simon had a doctor with him, a man nearly as tall as himself but thin as a pole, bald and with deep-set dark eyes. He asked her questions which she tried to answer.

No, she hadn't had a migraine for years, she told him. Yes, she added, she had taken a double dose of pills.

'Pills? What on earth for?' Simon asked abruptly.

Kate stared at him, but his face seemed to be receding and coming forward in a strange watery state. She blinked. 'Miss Stern told us . . .'

'Miss Stern?' Simon exploded crossly. 'I should have warned you. She lives on pills.'

'You've been feeling quite all right otherwise?' the doctor probed gently.

'Yes . . .' Kate began, and hesitated. 'No, to be honest, I haven't. I've been feeling desperately tired, but I thought it was the rush and . . .'

'She's been emotionally tired,' Simon Ellison interrupted again. 'She's had to uproot herself and her family from the snug little nook she had made for them, and she's scared stiff that she's done the wrong thing.' His words were hard but his voice was amused.

'It was Jerome's decision,' Kate began.

'Oh yes?' Simon asked. 'Don't tell me that he would have made it this way if you'd been against it.'

The doctor straightened. 'Miss Bayliss oughtn't to fly to Papeete tomorrow, Simon. I think she needs a few days' rest in bed.'

Kate tried to sit up, but found herself too weak. 'I don't want to be a nuisance. I'll be all right tomorrow . . .'

The doctor hesitated. He smiled at her. 'Well, we'll see. I guess I can come round first thing tomorrow and see how you are. Now I'll give you something to make you sleep.'

'That's all I need,' Kate said desperately. She looked at Simon and for a moment her vision was clear. She saw the tall, lean, good-looking man surveying her with a thoughtful, rather ironic smile. 'I'm sorry, Mr . . . I mean Simon,' she said.

He smiled. 'So am I, but it's just one of those things.' The doctor had been to his bag. Now he came to give her an injection.

'See you in the morning,' he said, and at last she was alone.

She turned her face miserably to the wall. Why had she to be sick at a time like this? It would merely add to Simon Ellison's dislike of her, for anything that was an obstacle to him became a nuisance.

In the morning, she awoke to see the sun streaming into the room. Nancy came to see how she was. Perched on the bottom of the bed, she told Kate she'd missed the most wonderful evening.

'Simon took us to the Clarendon and we saw all the film stars. He dances divinely, Kate — Simon, I mean. We're flying to Papeete today. Will you be all right?'

'I must be,' Kate said firmly. She got up, showered and dressed and was waiting when the doctor came.

'Well, you certainly look better,' he said cheerfully. He told her his name was Harry Moncrieff, and he agreed reluctantly that she could travel to Papeete, but that when she got there, she must take things quietly. He gave her some pills to take, but said he did not think she would find the flight tiring.

How wrong he proved to be! Even as Kate went with the others to the plane, she thought with dread of the five or six hours' flight that lay ahead of them. But she had to go. She simply had to go. Otherwise Simon would be annoyed, and . . .

The plane took off and the towering white skyscrapers became toy models in the distance, but by then Kate knew that she should have stayed behind.

Jerome and Simon were kindness itself, but it seemed an endless flight, and Kate longed to die as the plane dropped in air-pockets and droned on, people's voices bombarding her. But at last the plane landed, and Kate felt Simon lift her effortlessly in his arms and carry her down the gangway. Even in her misery, she felt the soft warm air caressing her cheeks, and smelled the delicious fragrance around her. She kept her eyes closed so that she need not thank Simon for what he was doing, and she wished with all her heart that she did not need his help.

She opened her eyes in the silence that followed after she had felt herself laid on a bed.

But Simon was still there, wearing a thin tropical suit, his face grim, his mouth a thin line.

'Why can't you act like an adult, Kate?' he said crossly. 'And admit how ill you feel. It would have been much wiser to have left you in Los Angeles.'

'I'm sorry . . .' she began.

He was not listening. 'Kate, I want no arguments. I haven't time to waste. We're going to the island today, but you're staying here for a week and then I'll fetch you.'

'A week!' Kate cried in dismay. 'But I'll be all right in the morning, and . . .'

'That's what you said yesterday.' He towered over her and frowned. 'You're a stubborn creature. Stop fighting. You can't win.'

'But Mike . . .'

Simon jerked a chair forward and straddled it. His voice was grim. 'Stop fooling yourself, Kate. No one is indispensable. Neither are you. Mike won't suffer because you're not around to fuss over him. It may even do him good to stand on his own two feet for a change. The family can manage without you. Maybe make 'em appreciate you the more. You need a long complete rest, and you're getting it, like it or not.'

He stood up with his usual quick impatient movements.

'A very good friend of mine, Georgia Appleby, will look after you. I'll send her in later, but first say good-bye to the family.'

Kate dared not trust herself to speak, she was so afraid of bursting into tears. Jerome and Mike solemnly filed into the room, looking at her worriedly.

'You'll be all right, Kate,' Jerome said, more as if to reassure himself than to comfort her.

Mike clung to her hand tightly, and Kate was aware that Simon was watching him with a frown. 'You will be all right?' Mike asked worriedly.

'Quite all right, darling,' Kate said quickly. She knew Mike's problem. He could still remember his mother's death, and when anyone in the family was ill, Mike always had this fear that the worst might happen again. 'I just need a rest.'

Nancy bounced in gaily. 'What you're missing, Kate,' she said cheerfully. 'Papeete is beautiful — palm trees everywhere and the most gorgeous-scented flowers, and the girls have long silky black hair and . . .'

'Time to go,' Simon said curtly, shepherding them like an impatient farmer out of the room. He came back to look down at Kate. 'Now, Kate, relax. Just forget the family and lead your own life for a few days. Everyone will be taken care of.'

Despite the sternness in his voice there was a kindness that startled Kate. Maybe he was human after all, she thought, as she stared up at him.

'I'm sorry I'm such a nuisance, Simon,' she said awkwardly.

He did not smile. 'You are, but it's not your fault. You can help me most by getting well. And I mean really well this time.'

He closed the door, and she was alone. Horribly, desolatingly, frighteningly alone. A whole week before she saw them again. A whole week. Seven long lonely days.

CHAPTER THREE

Simon's friend Georgia Appleby proved to be a friendly American woman.

She came to stand by Kate's bed, her eyes bright with curiosity.

'My, you poor girl!' she said with her American twang. 'You do look miserable. Simon wants me to take good care of you, and I guess I'll have to.'

'I'm . . .' Kate began and, to her dismay, found she was nearly in tears.

If Georgia noticed, she gave no sign. She turned away and said cheerfully, 'First thing is something nice to eat, and then the doctor's coming along to give you something to make you sleep. We'll have you up and about in no time at all.'

But it was three days before Kate woke up properly from the deep sleep of exhaustion and found herself curious as to this new world in which she was.

Georgia, who was in her late forties but

had the body of a girl twenty years younger, beamed.

'You'll just adore Papeete,' she said brightly, patting her beautifully-arranged amber-coloured hair. 'We call it the Paris of the Pacific. I came here fifteen years ago for a holiday and never left it.'

'You're so happy here?' Kate asked wonderingly.

Georgia laughed, a deep throaty noise. 'You'll be, too.'

Georgia drove Kate round the island. It had a fascination all its own. Never had Kate heard so much music, so much laughter, seen so many beautiful faces.

Georgia showed her the coral reef strip that extended into the Auae Lagoon on which the jet planes landed, and told her of the tremendous difference it had made to Papeete.

'People have always loved coming here, but today we are getting more and more tourists,' she explained.

Looking at the yachts slowly rocking in the harbour, and the masts of the schooners that brought the copra from the other islands, filling the air with the sickly scent, Kate asked a question.

'Is that a good thing?'

Georgia's long thin face looked ironic. 'It

50

is and it isn't. In many ways, it's spoiling things, for the Polynesian is changing fast as a result. On the other hand, they must eat, and copra and phosphorus and all the other means they have of making money have become very difficult. Undoubtedly tourism is needed by Papeete, but . . .' She turned impulsively to Kate. 'What are Simon's plans for the island?'

Kate hesitated, looking at the red spires of the churches and the brightly coloured houses along the quay and at the great mountains behind, towering high above them, the tops hidden in clouds.

'He said he was going to make it a centre for tourists. My stepfather is an architect and is going to design the hotel, I imagine. I don't know much about it . . .'

'Simon isn't one to talk,' Georgia agreed.

They drove along the quay, which was crowded with girls in bright red and yellow print dresses, with wreaths of flowers round their necks, or a flower thrust behind an ear, the great crimson or cream blossoms showing up against their dark silky hair.

'This is the Quai de Commerce,' Georgia said as she drove slowly, partly from choice, and partly to avoid knocking down one of the hundreds of happy-go-lucky cyclists and scooter-riders that swarmed everywhere.

'Here in Papeete we talk French, but on your island, it will be English. Great-Aunt Adèle disapproved strongly of everything French,' Georgia chuckled. 'Said it was immoral!'

'You knew her?' Kate asked eagerly.

Had she ever seen such green grass or such blue water? This was a fantastic land of sweet scents and tropical flowers, and everywhere she looked were palm trees, thousands of them, their feathery fronds moving gently in the breeze that made the hot day bearable.

Georgia laughed again. 'No one actually *knew* her — but she was quite a character. Very eccentric; she acted and expected to be treated as a queen. Which she was — to her islanders. I'm worried about Simon's plans, Kate, for on his island the people are different. I guess it can't last for ever, but it seems a shame to spoil them.'

'You think it will?' Kate asked, gazing up at the huge creamy flowers on a tree they had passed. The sweet sound of someone playing a guitar drifted on the air and the scent of deep trumpet-shaped flowers teased her nostrils.

'I'm afraid so. That's our so-called progress!'

Georgia relaxed, driving along the winding road below the mountains, pointing out to Kate some of the big thatched, open-sided houses.

'Most of those are owned by wealthy Americans who come here for holidays and stay a lifetime — like me,' Georgia said with a laugh. 'The spell Tahiti casts is subtle and lasting.'

'But what is it about it . . . ?'

Georgia shrugged. She waved her hand airily.

'Everything, I guess.'

She slowed up as a group of islanders came along the road, singing softly, haunt-ingly. The girls were tall and graceful, wear-ing vividly coloured *pareus,* so like sarongs, their dark shining hair falling to their waists, wreaths of white, scented flowers hanging round their necks. Some were playing guitars, all were singing. Several men were with them, tall, lean and moving with the same grace. They smiled and waved at the car as Georgia drove by.

'That's what I mean,' Georgia said. 'They're so happy. It's such a wonderful casual way of living. Nothing is important but happiness. There are three moods in Tahiti, Kate. The Polynesian lives in the present, he couldn't care less about the past or the future. They think we're crazy the way we worry if we miss a boat or oversleep. They don't think it matters. I'm beginning to think they're right.' She gave her deep throaty chuckle.

She slowed up again as they came to a lagoon. They could see the great waves rolling in and breaking against the distant reef, but here in this gentle lagoon, surrounded by palm trees slowly moving in the slight breeze, a long row of men were standing on the black lava sands, slowly hauling up their nets full of fish, shouting to one another. There were groups of women seated on the sands, clapping their hands in rhythm as they cried with joy at the fish that were being poured out of the nets in a throbbing mass.

'I wonder how Simon's going to cope with the Tahitian philosophy,' Georgia went on as she drove past the happy crowd. 'They're a people who live, as I said, for today. They're very ashamed for things they forget to do, not the things they do. I guess it depends on the way you see things, but they think making a noise when someone is asleep, or forgetting to wear a clean dress when visiting you, are terrible crimes.'

They were driving by a garden which ran down to the water's edge, covered with tangled masses of red and yellow flowers and oranges and fruit of every kind.

'What will really get Simon, who is, one must admit, a very impatient man with little use for fools,' Georgia went on, 'is the Polynesian attitude called *fiu*. It means "I'm fed up" or "I'm tired of doing this." When a Polynesian feels that way, he just packs up and vanishes, even if the job is half done. Even Simon's Great-Aunt Adèle had to learn to accept this. I wonder if Simon will . . .'

'You said you knew his aunt?'

'I met her often, but never really knew her. She never left the island, but she used to give wonderful parties — all strictly protocol and proper, of course, but they were great fun. I hope Simon will do the same when he gets settled in.'

'You've known Simon a long time?' Kate asked.

They had come to the end of the road. Now the mountains towering above them ran down straight into the water, and Georgia turned the car, driving them back towards the hotel.

'Only since he came out in December. His great-aunt died at the age of ninety and was still as strong as an ox. We were surprised when she died, for she seemed eternal, like the Pacific. Simon came out and we had that dreadful cyclone . . .' She shivered. 'We escaped it here, but his island got it badly.'

They were nearly back at the hotel when Georgia asked abruptly, 'Have you known Simon long?'

'Just over two weeks,' Kate said.

Georgia turned her head, looking startled. 'I got the feeling you were old friends. He was very concerned about you.'

'He was?' Kate asked, her voice disbelieving but her cheeks suddenly hot. 'Only because it upset his carefully planned schedule — my being ill, I mean,' she went on. 'No, I hardly know him at all. Why, I've only seen him . . .' She thought for a moment and then smiled at Georgia. 'Three times,' she said. Was that all? How was it that after three meetings, she felt she knew so much about Simon? His impatience, his ruthlessness, his amusement at her discomfiture?

'The first time I met him was when we went to see him about Jerome's job. Simon wanted to see me about it. Then . . . then I was ill in Los Angeles . . . and that day here when they left for the island. Three times.'

'How did your stepfather get the job?' Georgia asked, carefully parking the car alongside some of the other huge luxurious-looking American cars before the hotel.

'Simon heard of him as an architect and liked his views, so Jerome took me to see him.'

Georgia was getting out of the car gracefully despite her tight green skirt. 'So Simon didn't actually engage Jerome until he'd met you?'

'No, but . . .' Kate began.

Georgia wasn't listening. She was looking at her watch.

'I'm going to have a quick shower. What say we meet for a drink before dinner? See you?'

'Yes,' Kate said, going up to her bedroom at once.

She stood for a long time on her balcony. There was a wide sweeping view of the harbour and the wild Pacific Ocean beyond with its huge rollers racing in.

Had she only seen Simon three times? Kate thought. The railing of the balcony was hot under her hands, the sun beating down on her. The sweet sickly scent of the island drifted towards her, faintly she heard music and laughter.

Georgia was right. The island had a fascination. Everything was so different. What was the word her mother used to say wistfully? Gracious. That was it — a gracious way of living. Surely this was the most gracious way of all? A perfect climate, great beauty, delightful scents and laughter and happiness. Surely they would find happiness here, all of them?

The hotel was obviously an expensive one, and as Kate went to meet Georgia for drinks she thought worriedly of what this must be costing. Simon would probably insist on paying for it, but was that really fair? She hated the thought of being under an obligation to him — yet could Jerome afford to pay for it? Could she?

Everywhere she looked there were elegantly-dressed women laughing and talking to good-looking Polynesians or plump well-to-do American men. There was a feeling of gaiety, of money, of holidays.

Would they still feel the same happiness here if they had to work for their livings? Would she and Nancy be happy on the island, working for Simon? He would be a hard and demanding taskmaster.

Georgia waved to her, and Kate crossed the beautifully-furnished lounge to join Georgia on the patio, overlooking the blue Pacific.

'D'you like Simon, Kate?' Georgia asked abruptly after the white-clad waiter had served them.

Kate was startled. Her hair fell forward

over her face and she tossed it back with a quick movement of her head, so that she could see Georgia's face.

'Like him?' Kate stalled for time.

Georgia was smiling. 'Yes, like. I didn't say love!'

Kate felt her cheeks hot. She smoothed down the soft green silk of her frock to avoid looking into Georgia's frankly curious eyes.

'You want the whole truth?' Kate asked lightly.

Georgia chuckled. 'Yes, and nothing but the truth, but not if it'll embarrass you. I guess it wasn't a tactful question.'

'It doesn't embarrass me,' Kate said. 'It's just that . . . well, to be honest, Georgia, I don't like him.'

Georgia looked startled. The diamonds round her neck sparkled, her beautifully groomed hair shone. 'You don't like him?' she repeated slowly.

'No. Maybe I shouldn't say this, Georgia, for he's been most kind to us, but I always have a feeling he finds me childish, naïve and not a very nice person. He seems to treat me . . . to . . .' She sought for the right words. 'I feel he's patronizing me.'

Georgia looked puzzled. 'But why should he?'

Kate shrugged. 'I don't know. Maybe I'm

wrong — maybe I started off on the wrong foot with him. He thinks . . . he thinks I bully my family and that I'm selfish and . . .' She stopped speaking, for Georgia was frankly amazed.

'You're out of your mind, Kate. I'm sure he doesn't think that of you.'

Kate shrugged again. 'Maybe I am, but that's the way he makes me feel. As if I'm . . .'

'Poison ivy?' Georgia suggested with a smile.

Kate laughed. 'Exactly. I never appear at my best with him. Each time we've met I've either been terribly tired, or ill.'

Georgia stopped laughing. 'Maybe he'll be different on the island, Kate. After all, you can't be tired or ill all the time, can you? Or can you?' she asked with a burst of laughter.

When they stopped laughing, Georgia spoke more seriously. 'Frankly, Kate, I've an idea Simon is anti-female. Have you the same?'

Kate nodded. 'He told me he thought that romantic love was commercialized and greatly overrated and caused more misery than anything else. He told me he steered clear of it.'

Georgia leaned forward, her face interested. 'He told you that, and you've only seen him three times? How did you get on the subject?'

'He wanted to know if Nancy and I were engaged, and I said we weren't, and then he talked about love.'

'H'm. I don't mind saying that when he came here quite a few female hearts fluttered, Kate, but they got nowhere with Simon. He can be charming, but oh, boy, can he give them a neat brush-off!' Georgia chuckled. 'But even the wariest of men has an Achilles heel. I wonder where Simon's is? There are some beauties on his island. Caterina . . . that's odd, Kate. Her name is like yours. She's the most beautiful woman I've ever seen, and elegant and intelligent into the bargain. I guess Simon will meet his match there. By the way, Kate, I've made an appointment for you tomorrow at the beauty parlour.'

Kate's hand flew to her hair. 'I shampooed it,' she said.

Georgia nodded. 'I know, but being off-colour has made your hair dank and lifeless. You're getting the full works tomorrow — and Kate . . .' She paused for a moment and gave a singularly sweet smile. 'Do me a favour, Kate, and be my guest. It's not often I meet a girl like you.'

'Why, Georgia,' Kate was embarrassed, 'it is good of you. I've never had my hair done properly or . . .'

Georgia laughed. 'There always has to be a first time!'

The next day as Kate left the beauty parlour, she stared in the mirror in amazement. How right Georgia was. She had needed the treatment. Now her hair swung gently, its blondeness highlighted. They had curled the ends of her hair slightly and it made it look much silkier. Her skin looked brighter. She felt — different.

There was still so much for Georgia to show her on the island — the great beaches, some golden, some white, others the black powder of old lava. She watched the elegantly-clad tourists as they sunbathed or swam in the elaborate pools, the children of the Polynesians splashing like young porpoises in the country lagoons. Everywhere she heard soft music and laughter and met smiling faces, and she loved the way small children ran to greet them when they got out of the car at any place.

In the evenings, Georgia took her to the different night clubs that had sprung into being in the recent years; introduced Kate to many people, but always saw that she went to bed early.

'You certainly look a new girl,' Georgia said proudly as they sat in the hotel waiting on the final day for Simon to arrive.

'Thanks to you,' Kate said warmly.

Trying to relax, to ignore the tenseness that filled her, Kate realized that for the whole of the week she had stopped worrying about Mike and Nancy. For a moment, she felt conscience-stricken. How could she have forgotten them? Her old anxiety rushed back to her — had Mike been able to eat the local food? Was the water good or should it be boiled? Had he remembered to sleep under the mosquito netting? He had a horror of being enclosed — suppose he got badly bitten by mosquitoes . . . ?

'I'm going to miss you, Kate,' Georgia said, her voice wistful.

Kate looked at the well-dressed woman with the friendly eyes. 'I'll miss you, too,' she said honestly. 'I can never thank you enough. You've given me a wonderful week.'

'My pleasure,' Georgia said warmly. 'Maybe you can talk Simon into inviting me to the island one day?'

'I'm sure he would,' Kate said. 'I'd love the family to meet you. Nancy's so pretty . . . you saw her, didn't you, though? I forgot.'

'Just for a few moments. I wouldn't call Nancy pretty, Kate. She's cute — with that air of wide-eyed innocence and her youth and gaiety — but she's nothing like as pretty as you.'

'Me?' Kate was really surprised.

Georgia nodded. 'You have a lovely face, Kate. There's an air of serenity about you and your eyes are beautiful. Don't ever get an inferiority complex about your looks. You can hold your own with any woman.'

Kate went on staring at her. 'You're not serious?'

Georgia nodded. 'I most certainly am not kidding, Kate. Look, remember one thing. You're a pretty girl and you're intelligent. Don't let any man make you feel just a dumb bunny.'

Kate began to smile. 'You mean like . . .'

'Simon? Exactly.' Georgia looked complacent and turned her head, her face changing. 'Talk of the devil and here he is. The one and only Simon.' There was sarcasm and also affection in her voice as she spoke.

Kate caught her breath and felt her newly-won confidence fast disappearing. The tall lean man in a white tropical suit came striding impatiently across the lounge, towering above the other people, seeming to slash a pathway through the crowd.

'Georgia, you've certainly done a good job!' he began as he turned to look enquiringly at Kate. She coloured under his keen scrutiny and wondered at the surprised look on his face. 'You certainly look different.'

'I'm myself again,' Kate said.

'I'm very glad to hear it.' He turned back to Georgia. 'What did the doctor say? Okay for her to travel?' He spoke as if Kate was not there, or as he might have spoken about some child too young to answer for herself.

'He said I'm fine,' Kate began, but Simon ignored her, asking Georgia where Kate's luggage was and saying that he wanted to get away at once.

'I want us to get going before the wind changes, for I don't want this girl to be sick again,' he said, his voice almost curt.

'I'll send the luggage down to the Quay,' Georgia told him. 'It'll be there as soon as you are. I'll say good-bye now, Kate my dear.' She kissed Kate warmly and patted her on the arm.

'Take care of yourself, my dear, and I guess I'll see you again one day. By the way, remember what I said and never forget it. 'Bye, Simon. Be seeing you . . .' she said, and was off across the lounge, moving briskly and gracefully in her amber-coloured suit.

Simon was gazing at Kate curiously. 'What is it you mustn't forget?'

Her cheeks were hot. How could she tell him the nice things Georgia had said about her looks? 'I forget,' she muttered.

'Already? Not a very good memory, I'm afraid,' he said dryly. 'We'd better get cracking. We can walk down. It's quite close.'

The heat hit Kate as they left the shelter of the hotel. She wished she had worn flatties rather than the elegant high-heeled shoes. She tried to keep up with Simon's long stride. The sun blazed in her eyes and she was soon breathless. Simon strode ahead, completely oblivious of her, and suddenly Kate tripped. She nearly fell headlong, saving herself in time by clutching at the first thing that was handy. It happened to be a man's arm.

A man whose eyes were like sockets in his unhappy face, and with thinning dark hair. A man who cried out with surprise and angry dismay and turned to look at Kate as she regained her balance.

'I'm sorry,' Kate gasped. 'I nearly fell . . .'

'So did I,' he said sourly. 'You nearly knocked me over.'

'Something wrong?' Simon asked. He must have heard their voices and turned back. He was frowning.

'N-nothing,' Kate said. 'I stumbled and nearly fell and almost . . .'

'Knocked me over,' the unfriendly man said.

Simon was staring at Kate. 'You're breathless,' he said accusingly.

Stung into a retort, Kate said: 'You walk too fast.'

'I'm in a hurry,' he told her. 'As you know.'

Before she knew what was happening, he had scooped her up in his arms and was carrying her down the small pier.

'Simon . . . please,' Kate said quickly.

'It's easier and quicker this way,' he said curtly.

Kate lay still, conscious of the curious eyes of people they passed, the smiles they exchanged as they saw the tall handsome man carrying a girl in his arms. The pier was crowded with people, but Simon strode along, and almost miraculously a pathway opened before him.

When they reached the end of the pier and she saw the boat, which was smaller than she expected, Kate's heart sank, but she said nothing.

As it happened her fears were groundless, for the three-hour trip was perfect. They sat on deck and drank coffee and hardly talked, but Kate did not mind as she watched the incredibly blue translucent sea and looked at the islands with their towering jagged mountains, their vivid green trees, glimpses of pastel-shaded houses. It was all so beautiful. She thought again with a sense of shame how little she had worried about the family during the past week. She had been completely selfish and had lived in a world by herself.

'How's Mike?' she asked suddenly.

Simon turned to look at her. 'Fine. Shouldn't he be?'

Kate coloured. 'Of course, but . . .' She was startled by Simon's aggressive tone.

'You didn't expect him to be all right? Because you weren't there?'

'Of course I expected him to be all right, but . . .'

'There was always the chance, of course.'

Kate bit her lip. Why must Simon be so difficult? She drew a long deep breath, praying for patience and the right words. 'Georgia told me that sometimes when you first go to tropical lands, you suffer from . . . from . . .'

'Dysentery? Malaria — elephantiasis? Take your choice,' Simon said airily, lighting himself a cigarette. 'True, you can, if you're stupid. I'm not, so we don't. Our water is perfect, our food well cooked and in clean dishes, and we sleep under mosquito nets. Mike is fine. He's put on weight and got some colour in his pale cheeks. Nancy is having the time of her life, and as for your father, I mean stepfather, well, he's in paradise.'

'I'm glad,' Kate said.

Simon looked at her, his thick bushy eyebrows lifted. 'Are you?'

'Of course I am. Why shouldn't I be?'

'I just wondered,' he said, flicking the ash off his cigarette and looking away from her as he did so. 'After all,' he said slowly, 'you weren't there.'

There was a long silence as she tried to puzzle out what he meant. When she thought she understood, the quick anger mounted inside her. Was he implying that she believed the family were only well and happy if she was there to make them so? If he thought she believed that, then — then what sort of person must he think her?

'Simon . . .' she began.

He was not listening. He was walking across the deck to the railing. Behind them went on the usual noises of a small boat at sea — the shouts, the sudden ring of a bell, the laughter . . .

There was a faint smudge on the horizon.

'There's the island, Kate,' said Simon, and there was a new tense but happy sound in his voice. 'See it?'

She went to stand by his side and watched as the smudge grew larger and larger and she could see more clearly. There were twin peaks, one at either end, that seemed to shoot up towards the blue sky as if trying to outgrow one another.

'Mora Popaa, they call the island,' Simon said, his voice thoughtful. 'It has another name, but this means the Wise White Man. It was named after my great-aunt.'

'She lived here a long time?' Kate asked, watching the way his face had changed, become almost gentle as he gazed at the island they were approaching.

'Over seventy years,' he said. 'Seems incredible, doesn't it? Yet from the diaries she left behind, she was a happy woman. She had plenty of money and it was the sort of life she liked. It was quiet, she had friends who visited her, she loved to design gardens and to paint. She had people who loved and served her loyally.'

'She was . . . a widow?' Kate asked, a little uneasily, for although he was being friendly at the moment, she was afraid he might suddenly change.

Simon leant on the rail and nodded, his face sad. 'Yes. She was only married for about six months. She was the black sheep of our family. I had only heard of her vaguely until she died and left me the island. When she was seventeen, she fell in love with a man her parents refused to let her marry, so she ran away with him. In America they got married and then they came on here — or rather, to Papeete. In those days, it was very different. While they were there, William Scott, her husband, who was an unknown artist, died. It was a short illness, barely twenty-four hours. I've read some of her diaries. She was very bitter about it, blaming her parents for forcing them to leave England. She firmly believed it was the tropical country that had killed him.'

'How awful for her! Why, she couldn't have been more than eighteen,' Kate said thoughtfully.

'Fortunately Scott was a wealthy man with a private income. In addition, she later inherited money from a grandmother, the only member of her family who sympathized with her. She never wrote to the family or they to her. I had a shock when I learned she had left me the island. I didn't know she even knew of my existence. The solicitors told me she had instigated inquiries about her family and found that I, like her, had defied my parents, so I suppose she thought we had something in common.'

Kate's interest was too great for her to be cautious. 'You defied your family . . . ?' she echoed.

Simon was smiling. 'I most certainly did. We've always been in the tobacco business, got big plantations all over the world — really big concerns. I was expected to carry on the tradition, just as my brothers were. My only interest in tobacco is to smoke it.' He laughed suddenly. 'Besides, I wanted a more interesting life. I like taking gambles, meeting challenges. I find the Stock Exchange is the place for that.'

'But how on earth did she get the island? Did she buy it?' Kate was watching the blur of the island come closer and take shape. Now she could see the mountains — the harbour — the coral reef with the palm trees.

'An old Polynesian chief learned of her sorrow and gave her the island to console her. He also gave her two of his children to look after, and they were still with her the day she died, but then they vanished.'

'A case of *fiu,* I suppose,' Kate said thoughtfully.

Simon turned round to look down at her. 'What do you know of *fiu?*'

'Georgia told me. She wondered how you . . .' Kate stopped in time. They were getting on so well for a change that it would be a shame to say anything tactless. 'She told me about the parties your great-aunt gave.'

'Yes, she loved being a hostess. The island misses her in many ways. What did you think of Papeete?'

'Beautiful and fantastic. Like something out of a dream. Completely different from anything I've ever seen,' Kate said simply.

'You'll miss the night life. I imagine Georgia introduced you.'

'She took me to night clubs. I wasn't very thrilled.'

His eyes were puzzled. 'Most girls love them.'

'It was hot and . . . and rather boring,' Kate said. She could not tell him the truth — that it would have been wonderful had she been with the right man, but she had found Georgia's friends either too young or too old.

'So you won't miss the night life on the island?'

'I'm sure I won't. I've never been used to it.' Kate was watching the island. Now she could see clearly the people gathered on the beaches — see the canoes going out in the small lagoon. 'What strange tall mountain peaks.'

'Yes. The islanders have a legend about them. The one on the left is a woman, the one on the right is a male. The wide plain keeps them apart just as an unfriendly family might do, and so it's said the mountains have reached up into the sky in the hope that one day they can lean towards one another and meet.'

'But mountains don't grow!'

Simon was laughing. 'Of course they don't, but in Polynesian folklore anything can happen.'

Now they were closer to the island and she watched as the boat steered its way between the gap in the reef. The lagoon was small and they moored at a short wharf.

Long-legged girls in coloured skirts, with black hair hanging down to their waists, and flowers tucked behind their ears, came to greet them, putting *leis* of white scented flowers round Kate's neck. And then Nancy was there, a gay Nancy with her hair hanging loose and wearing a yellow cotton frock with her bare legs in sandals.

'You're really well, Kate?' she asked. 'Hi, Simon,' she said casually. 'I got those letters down.'

'Good girl,' said Simon, his voice warm and friendly. 'The car here?'

'Yes, Taro drove me down. He's teaching

me to drive, Simon.'

'Well, you're not to drive alone until I've given you a test,' Simon said. 'Even on this quiet island, there are hazards.'

'I know. Taro was telling me.'

Kate walked silently between the two of them and looked round her curiously. She could see where the cyclone had struck the island — whole trees ripped out by their roots and tossed about carelessly, wooden buildings collapsed into flat mounds. A long cream Rolls-Royce was waiting with a Polynesian chauffeur in immaculate white uniform.

'Great-Aunt Adèle believed in things being perfect,' Simon said quietly.

Kate looked at him with a smile. 'Georgia told me that.'

The car drive along a winding road that took them round the base of one of the thin jagged mountains to a flat plateau where there were rows of palm trees lining the white beaches, and then they saw the house.

For a moment, Kate could not believe her eyes. It was a mansion, a long two-storied house with a wide verandah running right round it and a balcony above. It was painted white and the windows had canopies to keep off the sun. The garden was ablaze with flowers, great masses of crimson hibiscus, white frangipani, and as the car stopped before the house, Kate could smell the sweet fragrance.

'Show Kate to her room and round the place,' Simon said curtly. 'I'll be in the office, Nancy. There'll be some more letters to do.'

'See you later,' Nancy said cheerfully as he left them.

The hall was lofty and cool. A Polynesian maid in the incongruous-looking uniform of an English parlourmaid came to fetch the luggage and to lead the way up the gracious winding staircase to the broad gallery. Nancy talked gaily as they followed her.

'It's positively fab, Kate. I've never known such a life existed. Simon's such fun to work for — drives me like mad and keeps trying to catch me out!'

'How's Mike?' asked Kate, a little breathless as she hurried up the broad stairs.

'He's at school. He's fine. Made several friends already. And Jerome is in paradise!'

'That's what Simon said.'

Nancy paused, her hand on the rail, to look back at Kate. 'I've never known Jerome so happy,' she said with an unexpected note of seriousness. 'You're going to love it here, Kate. We all do.'

'You're working already?'

'Of course. Simon has a lot of business to do. I mean he's carrying on his English and American business from here. If only we had the telephone it would be much simpler, but . . .'

Kate's room was as lofty and almost, she thought in that first moment, as big as the hall. Huge french windows opened on to a balcony. The bed was wide and had a carved headboard from which was draped a huge mosquito net. The windows were screened.

'Mosquitoes are a nuisance,' Nancy said suddenly. 'But there's always got to be a fly in the ointment. Wait till you meet Adam and Ian and . . .'

She gave Kate no time to tidy herself but led the way round the big house. Mike and Jerome were sharing a room, but Nancy had her own room, very similar to Kate's. Nancy led the way back downstairs and showed Kate the huge drawing room with its silk curtains and tapestries on the wall and the gleaming glass ornaments and shining silver. Kate saw the dining-room with its heavy furniture, all mahogany, and then Nancy led the way to Simon's office.

'But he doesn't want to see me,' said Kate.

'I want you to see the office. He said show you everything,' Nancy said with a laugh. She opened the door, and Kate hesitated.

She could see Simon, and he was talking to a woman.

The most beautiful woman she had ever seen in her life.

'That's Caterina. She's nice,' Nancy whispered loudly.

Even as she spoke the lovely woman looked up and saw the two girls in the doorway. Her ash-blonde hair was swept back from a high forehead and twisted in a chignon on her neck, her skin was creamy, she had dark violet-blue eyes and now she smiled.

'You must be Kate . . . how odd that our names are so alike,' she said, standing up with an easy graceful movement and coming towards Kate.

In that moment, Kate saw that Caterina was not as young as she had first thought, but her body was slender and she moved with a dignified grace that made you stare at her. Her voice had an attractive huskiness too, and her smile was warm.

'Yes, isn't it odd?' said Kate, and then thought what a dull stupid answer it was.

Simon was frowning as if annoyed at the interruption, but Caterina ignored him.

'It was bad luck being ill just as you arrived,' she said sympathetically. 'You look fine now, but a bit tired. Don't overdo it,

Kate. It's hard in these tropical countries to assess your own capabilities. Anyhow, if you feel sick or off colour, just send for the doctor. That's me.'

'You?' Kate gasped.

Caterina laughed happily. 'Yes, I'm the doctor. Wait until you see our hospital. Great-Aunt Adèle was the most generous woman I know, and she gave me *carte blanche.* I'll be proud to show you around any time.'

Simon interrupted. 'Go and get unpacked, Kate, and then have a rest. I'll introduce you to the others at dinner tonight. Now, Caterina, I want you to explain . . .' He took the lovely, elegant woman by the arm and led her to the huge desk that was under the window, and Nancy went to a smaller desk where there was a typewriter.

Kate felt dismissed. She gave a quick look round the room, seeing the filing cabinets that lined the walls, and then she quietly left the room, finding her way back to her bedroom. Having a shower and then lying down on the bed, she felt suddenly tired and a little unhappy. She felt out of things, rather like the odd man. What a shame, as Caterina had said, that she had been ill at the beginning. This last week seemed to have helped Nancy assimilate herself into the new life, a life that so far Kate did not know how to share. Simon would not need both of them in his office. What on earth was she going to do with herself all day?

CHAPTER FOUR

Kate was in a deep sleep when Nancy woke her. Nancy had changed into a yellow silk frock, her hair was twisted up on her head, and her eyes were shining.

'Wake up, Kate,' she said impatiently. 'Simon doesn't like us to be late. And look at your frock! You've crumpled it.'

Fighting awake through sleepiness, Kate sat up. 'I didn't mean to go to sleep . . .'

'Simon said you'd be asleep. I said you'd never go to sleep in the daytime, but he was right, as usual.' She glanced at her wrist watch. 'Better hustle, Kate. Know where the bathroom is? You do? Good. See you downstairs, and make it snappy. We always have drinks in the drawing-room before dinner.'

She was gone before Kate could ask one of the many questions in her head. Where was Mike? Surely school didn't last as long as this?

She hurried to the bathroom and took one of the quickest baths of her life. Whatever happened, Simon mustn't be given the chance to be sarcastic at her expense. Soon she was in a simple dark green frock that fitted her perfectly. She brushed her hair and hurriedly made up.

She felt strangely nervous as she went downstairs and opened the door of the drawing-room and everyone looked at her. Simon saw her and came across the room. He wore a dark suit and a white silk shirt. He smiled.

'Come and meet everyone, Kate.'

The room had seemed filled with people at first sight, but now as Simon led Kate round, she saw that there were only two men, Nancy, Simon and herself.

'This is Adam,' Simon said as he introduced a broad-shouldered man with a serious face and dark hair.

'Glad to meet you, Kate,' Adam said, his eyes looking at her thoughtfully. 'I gather you're going to help me. I sure could use a good book-keeper, which Nancy says you are.'

'She's not working for a week,' Simon said quietly.

Kate turned to him in dismay. 'I'm perfectly well . . .' she began.

He looked at her. 'You may feel perfectly well, but we don't want you sick on our hands, and it takes quite a while to throw off the after-effects of your experience.' He led the way to where Nancy was laughing and joking with a tall, too-thin boy in taper-thin black trousers and a green velvet coat. His hair was long and fell forward over his face.

'Ian, my nephew,' Simon said, and there was an oddly tense note in his voice.

Ian looked at Kate and grinned. 'Hi!'

Simon looked at Kate. 'I know you don't like sherry very much,' he said thoughtfully. 'We have a rather special cool drink here. Like to try it?'

'Yes, please.'

Kate sat down and listened to the conversation which swirled round the room. Simon was near her, and when he turned, she asked the question that worried her.

'Is Mike still at school?'

Simon smiled, his eyes amused. 'Course not. He comes out about three o'clock and spends the rest of the day with his father. It means he's in the open air most of the time and Jerome likes having him around.'

'But his homework . . .'

'They don't do homework at this school.'

Simon paused as if waiting for her comment.

She kept silent, for she was beginning to recognize these moments of his, when he set little traps into which she usually fell.

After a pause he added: 'They do prep at the school.'

'I see.'

His eyes were narrowed as he looked at her. 'I wasn't surprised to learn you'd arranged correspondence lessons. Mike took what he had to Mr. Anatole and he's finding them useful, combining them with his own methods.'

'I don't want Mike to drop behind,' Kate said, once again on the defensive. 'It's hard to pick up when you go back to a normal school.'

Simon laughed. 'This certainly isn't a normal school by any means, so you could be right.'

The door opened and Jerome and Mike stood there. Mike looked hot and grubby in shorts and his shirt hanging out. He saw Kate and came towards her quickly.

'Are you really well, Kate?'

She kissed him lightly, uncomfortably conscious of the amused smile on Simon's face. She felt annoyed. Why had he this effect on her? After all, Mike was her young

brother. Was there something wrong in kissing him?

'I'm fine, darling.'

'Run and get cleaned up, Mike,' Simon
said sharply. 'Caterina's coming to dinner.'

Mike turned, his face excited. 'She is? Oh,
goody!' He turned back to Kate. 'I'm going
to be a doctor, Kate, when I grow up. Caterina said I'm already showing promise . . .'

'Hurry, hurry!' said Simon. He waited
until the boy had gone and Jerome had
come to kiss Kate and ask after her health
and then excuse himself while he went and
changed, then he said:

'Well?'

Kate looked at him. 'Well — what?'

Simon smiled. 'Looks as if I'm going to
win my wager. Now I only have to make
you happy and I've won.'

'Your wager?'

Simon nodded. 'You forget so quickly,
Kate. Remember, I wagered a thousand
pounds to your favourite charity as against
some unknown forfeit you'll have to pay,
that in six months you'll admit you did the
right thing in coming here . . . ?'

Kate studied his face silently for a moment. She did not smile. 'Of course Nancy
and Mike are happy,' she said quietly.

'Everything is new and exciting, but will it last?'

Simon's face was grave. 'It will.'

'I wonder,' Kate said thoughtfully. 'Nancy is like a butterfly — loving the sunshine and new sights.' She looked down at her hands. 'I hope she stays happy,' she added.

'And you — do you think you'll be happy here?'

Kate looked up at him, shaking her hair back with a little jerk. 'I shall — if I have enough to do.'

He smiled. 'You will have.' He stood up. 'In a week's time,' he added as he walked away from her.

Adam came to take his place. Kate liked the friendly smile, the easy way he spoke to her. 'Tough luck falling ill on the way out,' he said. 'Nancy's settled down amazingly well.' He was watching the pretty seventeen-year-old as he spoke. She was laughing at Ian, her face alight with laughter.

'She's very pretty, isn't she?' Kate said quietly, as she watched Nancy's quick movements.

Adam smiled. 'Enchanting is the word, but so very young.' He turned to look at Kate. 'I'm glad you're going to work with me, Kate. There's a terrific backwash of work that Simon wants cleared up. We're still in a muddle as regards Great-Aunt Adèle's commitments and that sort of trouble. Nancy says you love book-keeping.'

Kate laughed. 'Nancy exaggerates. I don't love it but I can do it. I never could learn shorthand, so I learned book-keeping instead.'

'You can type?' he asked anxiously, and beamed when she nodded. 'Good. I need someone like you. Simon monopolizes Nancy, so I can never get her to help me.' He stopped speaking as the door opened. 'Now there,' he said quietly to Kate, 'is what I call a truly beautiful woman.'

Kate agreed wholeheartedly as they watched Caterina greet Simon with her lovely smile, and walk down the room with him, her steps smooth and almost floating, her deep red dress long and slender, off the shoulders, while round her neck was a gleaming diamond necklace.

'She's a widow, but won't be for long, I guess,' Adam said quietly in Kate's ear. 'And she's a darling into the bargain. Kind, tolerant and incredibly intelligent. Even Simon can't get the better of her. They're always crossing rapiers, and she frequently wins.'

A gong sounded just as Jerome and Mike hurriedly arrived, Mike going straight to Caterina's side. Kate saw the softened look on Caterina's face as she spoke to the boy. Kate had a feeling that she and Caterina were going to become friends.

This thought continued all through the beautifully cooked and perfectly served dinner, for Simon had put her next to Caterina, who at first devoted herself to talking to Kate. Caterina was easy to talk to, and when the conversation at the table flagged, she tossed the conversational ball back and forth, to Nancy, Ian, Jerome, even to Mike, and to Adam as well so that soon she had them all talking and laughing together.

After dinner, Mike went off to bed with Jerome by his side. Nancy and Ian went to play table tennis, Adam excused himself, for he was studying, he said, and Kate found herself left with Simon and Caterina.

Kate was not sure when she first had a premonition that she was playing gooseberry. Caterina included her in the conversation, gave no sign that she wanted to be alone with Simon. Simon was the same, and yet Kate had the feeling that both Simon and Caterina were waiting — maybe counting the moments — until they could be alone.

Kate remembered what Georgia had said, that every man had his Achilles' heel, and Georgia had said that she didn't think Simon would be a bachelor for long. She must have been thinking of Caterina. So beautiful and so absolutely perfect for Simon. Brave enough to argue with him, intelligent enough to outwit him and lovely to look at. The kind of wife any man could be proud of . . .

Kate looked quickly at Simon, at his lean stern face that was now alight with laughter as he spoke to Caterina. It gave her a glimpse of a different Simon, a relaxed happy Simon who was not bothering to be sarcastic or dryly amused. Maybe, Kate thought, she annoyed Simon as much as he irritated her. It was a strange thought. And not a very pleasing one.

She stood up suddenly. 'If you won't think me rude,' she said to Caterina, 'I think I'll go to bed. I feel most absurdly sleepy, yet I dozed all the afternoon.'

Caterina smiled at her. 'The island has that effect on everyone at first. You'll soon get adjusted to it, Kate. Simon is right. Do nothing for a week and you'll be surprised how well you feel. How about coming over to the hospital tomorrow morning about eleven and having tea with me?'

'Thank you,' Kate said. 'I'd like that.'

Simon was on his feet as if trying to hurry

her away. 'I'll arrange for the car to take you.'

Kate had got halfway up the stairs when she remembered she had forgotten to ask what time breakfast was. She had no idea where to find Nancy or she could have asked her. Kate turned and ran down the stairs again, her feet silent on the carpet of the hall. The drawing-room door was ajar and Caterina's husky voice halted her.

'I think Kate has a lovely face, Simon. So dedicated for a young girl.'

'She's dedicated all right,' Simon said, his voice dry. 'One of those happy martyrs. She was sixteen when her mother died and she took over the management of the family and made them toe the line . . .'

Kate stifled a little shocked cry of pain and turned, running up the stairs and to her bedroom, closing the door, leaning against it. Foolish, stupid tears stung her eyes. Why did it hurt so much? So that was what he still thought of her! A bossy girl, bullying her family and enjoying it? Was that why he was always so sarcastic, why he seemed to delight in making her look a fool?

She brushed the tears from her face as she heard a gentle knock at the door. It was Jerome, his face concerned.

'And how's my Kate?' he asked, giving her

90

a big hug. 'We missed you, Kate. Missed you very much.'

Suddenly she was clinging to him, crying against his shoulder, hearing his puzzled worried voice as he tried to comfort and soothe her.

'There's nothing to cry about, Kate, my dear. Everything's working out fine. Just fine.'

Kate managed to dry her eyes and even smile as she apologized to him.

'This wretched illness has made me so stupidly weak, Jerome. I'm sorry . . .'

He smiled at her. 'I know, dear. Caterina and I were talking about you the other day. You took a heavy burden on your shoulders and did a fine job, too. Now you can relax, Kate. This is a very pleasant way of living. We have no financial worries, either. You'll see, Kate. I know everything seems strange to you just now, but . . . you'll see,' he repeated anxiously, as if trying to convince himself. 'Everything's just fine. Now, Kate, I came to look for you. Mike says what about coming to say goodnight?'

Kate dabbed her eyes with her hands and managed to smile. 'I'm terribly sorry, Jerome. I guess I'm still a bit weak, and . . .'

Jerome's face was worried. 'Maybe we shouldn't have come out here, and . . .'

Kate caught his arm impulsively. 'Oh, it's not that, Jerome. I think we did the best thing. It's a wonderful chance for us all. I'll be all right. It's just that — that the week has made such a difference. I feel out of things, a stranger.'

'My dear Kate,' he said, giving her a bear hug affectionately. 'A stranger? Don't talk nonsense. Now run along or Mike will be asleep. The air here makes one sleepy. You're having an early night?'

'I thought so,' Kate said as she opened the door.

'Good idea. See you tomorrow, Kate,' Jerome said.

Kate hurried down the passage to the big lofty room Mike shared with his father. Mike was lying on his back, hands folded under his head. He grinned at her.

'Hi!'

'Hi,' Kate said as she pulled up a chair. 'I just dropped by to say goodnight. How're things, Mike?'

'Fab, just fab,' he said with a grin. He sat up. 'Kate, what d'you think? Mr. Anatole — that's our teacher — says I've got brains, but I ought to use 'em more. He's not bad.'

'And the other children?' Kate asked a little anxiously, remembering past incidents when Mike had come home from school with a black eye or bruised face, struggling with the tears he was ashamed to shed. He had always been a frail, rather gentle boy, hating fights and trying to hide his fear.

Mike grinned. 'They're great, Kate, just great. Mr. Anatole wants to meet you.' He gave a terrific yawn. 'Gosh, Kate, isn't it great here? This is the bestest, the very bestest. I went swimming with Simon the other day, and it was so warm and the fish are all colours and the most weird shapes . . .' He gave another terrific yawn.

Kate stood up, bent and kissed him, tucking the white mosquito netting round him carefully. ' 'Night, darling,' she said softly.

Back in her own room she went to the window and looked at the dark night with the stars twinkling in the sky. A thin crescent moon shone. There were strange noises in the night and the gentle rustle of the palm trees moving in the breeze.

Everything would be all right, Jerome had said. Everything was all right — for Jerome, Nancy and Mike. She was the odd one out.

CHAPTER FIVE

Kate opened her eyes and blinked lazily as she saw the pretty Polynesian maid standing by the side of the bed, the breakfast tray in her hand.

Kate caught her breath. She must have overslept! What a chance for Simon to be sarcastic, she thought. She sat up hastily, brushing her hair out of her eyes and smiling apologetically at the Polynesian girl, whose long black hair looked so strange under the small frilled white cap, and on whose slender lithe body the old-fashioned uniform of an English parlourmaid seemed out of place.

'You shouldn't have bothered . . .' Kate began.

The girl gave a little bob. 'I am Tehutu,' she said. Her voice was slightly sing-song and pretty. 'My mission is to care for you.' She gave another little bob, went to the windows and drew back the curtains, turned to give Kate a searching but friendly look and then vanished.

Kate was surprised at the way she enjoyed her breakfast. Like all the meals she had had in the big house, it was delicious — exotic fruit and cereal, a boiled egg and then a gloriously crusty roll and butter. The coffee was very hot and strong. After Kate had slid the tray on to the bedside table, she relaxed for a moment in the bed. How she had slept, she thought, giving a relaxed yawn. She looked round the beautiful room and thought how very different it all looked from her small room in Ealing — how utterly different this new life would be.

And then she thought of Simon. She was out of bed instantly. Never had she showered and dressed so swiftly in her life. It was bad enough to have overslept and missed breakfast, but she must not give him the chance to accuse her of being lazy, she thought, remembering painfully the words she had heard the night before.

As she leant close to the glass to make up her face, she thought of the casual yet sophisticated elegance of Caterina. So very lovely and charming, with that husky voice and friendly smile. How nicely she had talked to Mike, never treating him as a child and something of a nuisance. No wonder

Simon . . .

Kate took a long deep breath.

Simon!

Would she ever forget the note in his voice as he had said to Caterina, 'Kate is one of those happy martyrs'? she wondered.

What else was it that he had said? Kate asked herself.

Oh, yes! He had said: 'She was sixteen when her mother died, she took over the management of the family and made them toe the line . . .'

Almost blindly, Kate walked to the window, opening it and stepping out on to the balcony. Had she made the family toe the line? she asked herself worriedly. Had she bullied them? Forced them to do things they disliked doing? Yet would she ever be able to forget the happiness on Jerome's face when he heard that she had agreed that they should have come out here? Kate brushed her hand across her eyes. It hurt terribly to know that Jerome might have refused this wonderful chance for him — because Miss Stern had told him enough to let her know just what a difference this could make to Jerome's future — if Kate had not agreed?

There was a delightfully cool breeze as she stood on the balcony. She stared round her. Never in her life had she expected to see such beauty. There were palm trees everywhere, thousands of them, climbing the mountains that towered above her, crowding down to the water's edge.

She glanced at her wrist watch and caught her breath with dismay. One last look in the glass. She did wish she looked older. Her oval face looked childish and the way her honey-brown hair hung straight and silky added to her naive look. She straightened the flat pleats in her simple white frock, glanced over her shoulder to make sure the seams of her stockings were straight, then took a deep breath and left her room.

As she walked down the graceful curving staircase lightly, she could hear the sound of soft singing somewhere and then the frantic click-clack of Nancy's typewriter. It was strange, Kate thought, what an effect Simon's personality had already had on Nancy. Nancy seemed delighted to work hard for him, and saw his strict demands as a friendly challenge. Kate caught herself envying her young sister. Simon's effect on her was . . .

She stopped dead, catching her breath, for Simon was in the hall below her, looking up, watching her every movement. For a moment, as she stared at the tall, lean man in the immaculate white shorts and open-necked shirt, long blue socks and white shoes, she saw him as an attractive man, and not as the disagreeable person he usually was to her.

And then she saw the quizzical smile in his eyes and the image of an attractive friendly man vanished.

'I'm sorry I overslept,' Kate said stiffly, walking down the stairs quickly.

'Don't apologize,' Simon began.

Kate was not listening. 'I'm afraid Tehutu brought me breakfast in bed. I could have got up . . .'

'I don't doubt it,' Simon said, his voice dry. 'The fact remains, Kate, if you'll let me get a word in edgeways, the custom here is for everyone to have breakfast in bed.'

Kate stared up at him, her eyes startled. He must be teasing her, she thought. And then she saw that he wasn't.

'You mean . . . you mean everyone has breakfast in bed?'

His smile appeared for a second, only to vanish. 'Yes, I mean precisely that. My great-aunt had one weakness — she loathed getting up in the morning, so she made it a rule that everyone should have breakfast in bed.'

'But . . .' Kate began.

Again he smiled briefly. 'It doesn't sound

like me? I agree. Normally I loathe eating in bed, but here, you'll find in time, everything is different. Besides, it makes things easier for the staff. Keeps us out of the way while they're working. What did you think of Tehutu's uniform?' This time he really smiled, and Kate smiled back.

'It looked . . . well, it looked comical on her.'

Simon nodded. 'I agree, but please don't tell her so, Kate. They're so proud of their uniforms. Come along and meet the staff,' he said, taking her arm in his hand.

His touch was light but warm as he took her through the luxurious drawing-room, opened the door of the big empty ballroom, telling her of the parties his great-aunt had once held, and showing her the table-tennis table.

'Nancy and Ian play every night — or else dance,' Simon said, showing her an old-fashioned gramophone on a table.

Still holding her arm as if afraid she would slip away at any moment, Simon showed Kate the vast kitchen, surprisingly cool and spotlessly clean.

Tehutu giggled and bobbed as Simon spoke to her and then a huge Polynesian woman with a flower tucked behind one ear and wearing a blue frock covered with a large, very starched apron, came forward with a smile for Simon and a quick curious look at Kate.

Simon waited and Kate felt embarrassed. Was she expected to say something appreciative? she wondered. She began apologetically:

'You must find us a nuisance. After cooking for Mrs. Scott — I mean, there are so many of us . . .'

The Polynesian woman's face was one huge happy grin as she looked from Kate to Simon and then back to Kate.

'*Aita peopea,*' she said gaily, and then laughed at the mystified look on Kate's face. 'That means it does not matter. You will learn soon — the way we talk. We are happy, I promise you. Very happy to have the house filled with *popae.*' She laughed again. 'That means — the white people. It is very good, too, to have young *vahines* here. *Vahines* is woman in our talk. When the old *vahine* died, our hearts felt like they were broken, we were so sad. No one to scold us, no one to praise us or for us to please — but now the house is filled with *vahines* and we are glad.'

'Fetia is right,' Tehutu spoke shyly. 'It is good you have come. *Aué* — we were afraid of *tupapaus.*' She looked over her shoulder

100

with a shiver. 'We thought they had come to punish us, and then the laughter came back and deep voices and everything was good again . . .' She bobbed again and looked at Simon and smiled shyly. 'We are happy that you are here.'

As Simon led Kate away from the kitchen, his hand tightened round her arm.

'You see what I mean, Kate?' he said. 'They hate quiet houses and loneliness. They like to have us here.'

He took her to a room she had not seen. He unlocked the door with a key and then stood back to let her enter.

'Nancy has never seen this room,' Simon said. 'She's too young to appreciate it.'

Kate was staring round the enormous room that she saw instantly was an artist's studio. Startled by the unexpected friendliness in Simon's voice, she enjoyed the implied compliment, but the next moment her elation vanished, for Simon was indicating the many paintings on the walls, and those on several easels.

'Take a look at them and see if you notice anything strange,' he said, his voice sceptical again.

Kate had been looking at the huge bay windows which seemed to embrace the blue Pacific ocean; staring at the fantastically large rollers as they raced towards the reef of the lagoon, there to break, throwing up great fountains of sparkling water. The palm trees were gently swaying in the breeze and it was incredibly beautiful.

The question, the tone of Simon's voice, all jerked her back from gazing at the beauty and for a moment she could not concentrate.

'I — I haven't had time to look,' she said quickly.

Simon's hand fell away from her arm and he stood back.

'Take your time. You'll probably soon notice it, for most people do.'

Her small white even teeth bit her lower lip for a second. What was he implying? she wondered. That if she could not notice the strange thing about the paintings, she must be sub-normal in intelligence?

Every nerve in her body was tense and conscious of the amused glance the tall man gave her as he followed her round the room slowly. They were colourful paintings — some dramatic, some merely pretty, others strange and bewildering as if the artist had been experimenting with colours. Kate felt despair creeping over her. Caterina would have been able to answer him at once, Kate felt sure of that. Was Simon at this moment comparing her stupidity with Caterina's wit and intelligence? Kate wondered. And then she suddenly realized what Simon meant.

Kate swung round triumphantly. 'She only painted trees and water and . . .'

Simon nodded, but his lean humorous face did not look very impressed. 'Exactly,' he said, his voice flat. 'She had an aversion to painting human beings, apparently. Look at this one.'

Kate went to stand by his side before the painting of a single palm tree, dancing in the breeze, its roots hidden in white sand and rock, behind it the sun-kissed blue sea.

'Painted with love,' Simon said, his deep voice changing, becoming warm. He waved his hand vaguely. 'I call these Great-Aunt Adèle's love letters. When she lost her husband, she transferred her love to the island. She was fortunate to be able to sublimate her love.'

For a moment his voice was wistful and Kate was startled. He had sounded almost envious of his great-aunt.

Simon went on, his voice deep and still warm, and Kate had the strange sensation that he had forgotten she was there and was merely thinking aloud.

'Her husband must have taught her the fundamentals of painting and she taught herself the rest by trial and error. She loved the island and refused to leave it. She had a resident doctor for when she was ill and had the hospital built. If she was lonely, which was rare, she invited people here. She would listen to them, learn from them what was going on in the outside world. She was complete in herself — together with the island. They called her eccentric.' Simon stared at Kate. 'Don't you think that maybe *we're* the eccentrics because we haven't yet found the right way to live?'

Before she could answer, Simon had led her to another painting. This one was of a grove of coconut palms, battered and beaten by wind and rain, one tree tossed into the air, its roots vainly clutching for the security of earth it had lost, its palm fronds limp with fear. Other trees were bent helplessly before a wind which Kate could almost hear screeching violently while everywhere rain fell mercilessly like a grey blanket.

'The island is not always peaceful,' Simon said slowly. 'It can be cruel and violent, but Great-Aunt Adèle still loved it.'

He showed Kate wide tall bookshelves in a small annexe.

'Help yourself when you want to read,' he said, his voice friendly but impersonal again as if he had dismissed the thought of his great-aunt. 'I'll give you the key to the studio.'

He took her to a wide mahogany desk by the window. It was a small window, and gazing out of it, Kate could see one solitary palm tree silhouetted against the blue water.

'This is where she wrote her diaries, Kate,' Simon went on. 'I think they'd make a fascinating book.' He smiled, his face lighting up. 'Fortunately most of the people she wrote about are dead, otherwise we'd be sued for libel! She had a cruel tongue and no use for hypocrites, but a warm heart for those in trouble.'

Rather like you, Kate thought quickly. What a strange man he was. His moods changed from one moment to the next. Now he was human, warm and friendly and she found it hard, glancing at him swiftly, to imagine him saying the cruel words he had said the night before about her. But then he was like his great-aunt and hated hypocrisy. Did he think her love for her family, her concern for them was all part of an act?

'Read them if you have time, Kate,' Simon was saying, opening a drawer and showing her the old volumes. 'I found them fascinating. About the primitive life on the islands, her attempts to anglicize the islanders and reform them.' He smiled. 'Poor

Great-Aunt Adèle — yet she had the courage and common sense to accept the fact that they could never change and still be happy, so she compromised and mixed her English way of life with theirs.'

'She must have been a wonderful woman,' Kate said quietly.

Simon's face was thoughtful as he looked at her. 'Yes. I only wish I'd known her personally. When you read those . . .' he pointed to the books, 'you'll feel as I do. They're vividly written — she seems to come alive.'

He glanced at his watch. 'Taro will be bringing the car for you in fifteen minutes and Caterina is expecting you at the hospital.' Again his voice had changed. He was formal, polite, even a little stiff. He locked the door of the studio and looked at Kate.

'I keep this room locked up as the young have no reverence for their elders,' Simon said crisply. 'I don't want young Ian in there messing around. Probably think it a fine joke to mess up the paintings . . .'

'Surely he wouldn't . . .' Kate was momentarily shocked.

'Wouldn't he?' Simon laughed shortly. 'You'd be surprised at what young Ian could do.'

Kate hesitated. What a hard note that was in Simon's voice, she thought. As if he disliked his nephew intensely. Yet Ian was very young, and . . .

Simon was holding out the key. 'Take care of it,' he said curtly. 'I don't want it lost.'

Her fingers closed tightly over the key. 'Of course I'll take care of it. Thanks . . . thank you very much.'

'I thought you might be interested and it'll give you something to do during this next week,' Simon said curtly. 'You do understand that the doctor prescribed another week's rest? I don't want any argument about it.'

Kate stared at him. He had changed again, she thought in amazement. Now he was the man she disliked so much.

'I won't argue,' she said quietly, and saw him give her a puzzled look. 'And thank you for trusting me with the key. I'll take great care of it and I shall enjoy reading your diaries.'

'I thought you would,' said Simon. 'You're the serious type. I'm sure you never read light books or thrillers . . . Well, I must be off. Mustn't waste any more time.' He touched Kate's arm lightly. 'Give my love to Caterina.' He hesitated. 'I hope the diaries will interest you, Kate. You see —' he paused and gave a brief flashing smile that lit up his whole face, 'I've got to find some way of keeping you happy here. You haven't forgotten our wager?'

'Wager?' Kate echoed, bewildered.

Simon laughed. 'Yes, our wager that you'll be happy here. I'm looking forward to collecting my forfeit!'

Kate remembered, then. He had promised to give one thousand pounds to her favourite charity if she could honestly say she was unhappy on the island after six months, and if she was happy, he was going to demand a forfeit in payment.

'What forfeit?' she asked warily.

Simon laughed again and for a moment looked young and human. 'I haven't thought one up yet, but trust me, I will!'

He was still laughing as he left her and she went up the stairs to her room, tightly clutching the key he had given her. She put the key at the back of the drawer of her beautiful walnut dressing-table and found herself half wishing that he had not given her the key. Supposing she lost it?

Shivering at the mere idea, she hastily brushed her hair and made up her face, looking wistfully at her reflection and wishing she had Caterina's sophisticated look, her elegance, that wonderful ash-blonde hair, that husky intriguing voice. How dull and naïve Simon must find her in comparison, Kate thought. If only she could think of witty things to say! Or look as beautiful as Caterina.

CHAPTER SIX

Taro, the Polynesian chauffeur, arrived punctually with the car. He was full of smiles and friendly chatter as they drove along a road lined with tall trees whose great scarlet flowers met overhead like wreaths. He was obviously very proud of the island as he pointed out the harbour where two schooners were moored on the incredibly blue water and several small boats were bobbing up and down, tugging at their buoys. It was the blazing colours everywhere that caught Kate's eye — the amazingly vivid reds and orange that Great-Aunt Adèle had captured so well on canvas. The car climbed the mountainside, passing trees laden with white and cream flowers whose strong scent filled the air. At last they reached the hospital — a single-storied, long white building whose glass windows sparkled in the sunshine like diamonds.

Kate was shown immediately into Caterina's room and, in a moment, Caterina joined her. But it was a new, strange, and oddly impersonal Caterina, very different from the friendly glamorous woman Kate had met the night before.

Caterina's hair was hidden in a white turban, she wore a tailored, short-sleeved white coat, white stockings and shoes. She had a stethoscope sticking out of her pocket and her voice, still husky, was brisk and authoritative.

'I'm afraid you've picked a bad day, Kate,' she said. 'Normally this is my quiet time, but we've had several casualties in today and I'm up to my eyes . . .'

Kate said quickly, 'I could come another day.'

Caterina smiled and indicated a chair before relaxing in a long cane lounge chair, tucking her feet under her skirt.

'Of course not. Do me good to sit down for five minutes,' said Caterina, with another quick but still impersonal smile. 'What do you think of the island?'

'Very beautiful indeed,' Kate told her warmly.

Caterina gave a little shrug. 'You'll either adore it or hate it here. Nancy seems to have adjusted herself well.'

'She certainly has,' Kate agreed quickly.

'But she's got plenty to do. I . . .' She leaned forward, her face earnest, 'I've always been used to a busy life. I just don't know what I'll do for the next week — must I really just relax?'

Caterina's eyes were thoughtful, her voice grave. 'Yes, Kate, you must. Simon told me you were one of those industrious people who can never let up . . .' She paused, her eyes still watching Kate's mobile face.

Kate caught her breath. She knew also that Simon had said other things about her — that she was a 'happy martyr' and had made her family 'toe the line'.

'I had no choice,' Kate said quickly.

Caterina nodded. 'I know, but now you have. That's the difference, Kate. You'll find you have a lot to learn on this island. One of the most important things is to adjust yourself to this very different way of life. I found it difficult. Only old Mrs. Scott, Simon's great-aunt, and her need of me, stopped me from rushing back to the rat-race of civilization. How thankful I am now that I stayed here.'

'Why did you come?' Kate asked as a young Polynesian maid brought in a tray of tea.

Caterina shrugged again. It was a pretty, graceful gesture, the way she did it. 'Why?

Why does a woman run away and hide herself? Because, like old Mrs. Scott, I had lost the man I loved. He had died. Without reason, I felt. He was a great man and could have done much good in the world. I was bitter, as Mrs. Scott was once, but she taught me how to make a new life here and now I am happy . . .' Her voice softened suddenly. 'I trust that you, too, will find happiness here.'

'But I'm not running away from the rat-race,' Kate began.

Caterina smiled. 'That I realize — but Jerome is, and I think he is wise. He has vision, too great to be destroyed by vandals. He is like Simon, a man of dreams.'

'Simon — a man of dreams?' Kate echoed in surprise.

Caterina sipped the tea in the delicate china cup slowly.

'But of course. I forget, you do not know him yet, Kate. When you do, you will realize that the man you see is not the real Simon. Do you like him?'

The question was unexpected and startled Kate. She felt her cheeks suddenly hot. She had been honest with Georgia, but some seventh sense warned her not to be the same with Caterina.

'I hardly know him,' Kate said quickly.

'He's very generous . . .'

Caterina smiled briefly. 'In Ian's language, you can say that again. All the same, he can be hard. We fight, often. You see, old Mrs. Scott trusted me and asked no questions. Simon trusts no one — least of all a woman.' She gave a little shrug. 'I do not know the whole story, of course, but I believe that once Simon was badly hurt by a woman and that explains much.' Her voice was warm and, to Kate, it sounded possessive.

Caterina went on, 'He takes his responsibilities so seriously. He could be a very wealthy man if he sold his right to the island, but he would not contemplate it. He desires to make the Islanders independent — to help them.'

'You think the idea of a tourist hotel is good for the islanders, do you?' Kate asked, putting down her cup. 'Georgia . . .'

'Georgia . . .' echoed Caterina, her voice amused and scornful. 'What does she know? Simon does not talk to her.' She stood up. 'I have work to do, Kate. Believe me when I say that Simon is doing a wonderful thing for the islanders, and they know it and respect him for it.'

She walked with Kate to the entrance, briefly introducing her to the friendly, white-haired Matron and two of the Sisters they met.

'We will meet again soon,' Caterina said with a brief smile, and turned away, hurrying back to the hospital.

Kate got into the car and Taro drove away swiftly as if glad to get away from the hospital. As he showed her waterfalls that fell thousands of feet in a straight line to churn creamily in pools where yellow lilies floated — as he slowed up to show her caves where huge ferns were sprayed with the water dripping from the low roofs and the strong scent of tropical flowers filled the air, Kate's thoughts were of Caterina.

She had been friendly and yet so very impersonal. Kate reminded herself that Caterina was a busy woman and a dedicated one. No doubt Simon would accept that, without adding sarcastically that she was a 'happy martyr'. How those words still hurt, Kate thought. Perhaps Simon had been joking, yet his voice had not sounded as if he was. Had he had an unhappy love affair? It was difficult to imagine him in love, to believe that any woman would — or could — hurt him.

Yet Caterina knew him well, that was obvious. The way she had dismissed Georgia. What was it Caterina had said? Kate asked herself. Oh, yes! 'Simon does not talk to her.' Meaning, presumably, that he did talk to Caterina!

A whole week of doing nothing lay ahead of her, Kate thought miserably. She would be bored to tears. And then she remembered the diaries. Simon had trusted her with the key — even if he had warned her not to lose it, at least he had trusted her with it. She would read the diaries and perhaps the time would not drag so much.

Kate turned suddenly to Taro. 'You're glad Mr. Ellison is building the hotels?'

Taro's handsome face looked startled. 'Of course. We are a happy people, but the hurricane was a bad thing. We have to eat, so . . .'

He slowed up the car at the edge of a precipitous drop where the mountainside fell away to the blue water below. The palm trees rustled their fronds gently in the sudden stillness. Far out in the ocean were the sails of some boats. Kate drew a long slow breath. It was a very beautiful place. Caterina had said that she would either love or hate it. Which would it be? Kate wondered.

Kate was surprised how quickly she adapted herself to her new leisurely life. Now that she could enjoy breakfast in bed without a sense of guilt she relaxed, enjoying the delicious meal and the knowledge that there was no need to rush to the bathroom, hurriedly cook the breakfast, get Mike off to school and Nancy to work, and then queue up for the bus on a cold wet street corner. Now she could bath slowly, dress and stand on the balcony in the welcome breeze — for the days were very hot — and then wander downstairs.

Sometimes Taro would come with the car and drive her round the island; or to the hospital where Caterina, in some of her few leisure moments, would welcome her and yet still be the different Caterina, the professional woman. Sometimes Kate would sit in the annexe to the studio and read old Mrs. Scott's diaries. As Simon had said, they made fascinating reading and showed vividly how primitive life on the island had been in those early days. Once Simon took Kate to the school where Mike was.

It was a surprise invitation, for Kate was sitting on the wide terrace, writing a letter to one of her friends in England, when she heard a firm familiar step on the polished tiles. She looked up to find Simon standing there, his khaki shorts and shirt damp from the heat.

'I'm just going to shower, Kate,' he said briefly. 'In ten minutes I'm going to the school. Like to come along?'

Kate was on her feet. 'Oh, I would.'

'Good. Don't keep me waiting,' Simon said abruptly, and turned away.

Kate hurried to her bedroom and quickly changed into a clean frock. The heat was so sticky that she changed her clothes several times a day. Miraculously Tehutu collected the frocks and returned them a few hours later, washed and immaculately ironed.

Kate chose a leaf-green frock of batiste material, that Miss Stern had recommended for wear in the tropics. She brushed her hair vigorously, wishing she was near the beauty salon to which Georgia had sent her. She made up carefully and then hurried down to the hall. She got there at the same time as Simon, now immaculate in white shorts and shirt, his short blond hair still wet from the shower.

He lifted his dark tufty eyebrows and smiled.

'Punctual! An unusual virtue in a woman.'

'Jerome considers it a failing,' Kate said, trying to speak lightly, 'because he's usually late.'

'Jerome has strange views,' said Simon, leading the way to the waiting car. 'But doubtless he'll change.'

Taro leapt to attention, very smart in his white uniform.

Simon helped Kate into the car with his odd mixture of impersonality and old-world courtesy. She tried to think of something to say to him. Although they met at meal times, it was odd, when she came to think of it, how little she and Simon had ever had to say to one another. Nancy, now, could chatter away to him and even tease him — Mike could talk happily, asking his perpetual questions — Jerome was always discussing plans and drawings, but Kate! Sitting silently beside Simon, Kate asked herself why she should still feel so ill at ease with him. Was it because they shared so few interests? When Caterina came to dinner, she led the conversation, gathering in the others skilfully, opening up new subjects, but then Caterina and Simon were old friends. Yet not so old, Kate realized. After all, Caterina had only known Simon since his great-aunt died.

'There's the school,' Simon said curtly.

Kate looked in the direction indicated and saw a large, thatched building built high on stilts. The sides were all open and she could see about thirty children sitting at small desks.

Simon helped Kate up the steep ladder and introduced her to the teacher, a tall bald-headed man with vivid blue eyes.

'This is Mr. Anatole,' Simon said, his lean

face relaxed in a friendly smile. 'Harald, this is . . .'

'Mike's sister,' smiled Mr. Anatole with his hand outstretched. 'I have heard so much about you.' His clasp was warm.

Simon smiled quizzically. 'Mike never stops talking about her,' he said dryly.

Harald Anatole looked disapproving. 'It is natural — why not? She has been father, mother, sister and guardian to the boy.' He turned to Kate. 'Mike is a fine boy, but his brain was allowed to be lazy. He was not happy in school?'

Very conscious of Simon by her side, Kate tried to explain. 'He . . . he was rather delicate and got bullied.'

Harald Anatole smiled sadly. 'That so often happens, but he must learn to overcome fear and defend himself. Here we have no bullying, but we teach self-defence. Have no fears, Mike will be all right.'

Simon spoke abruptly. 'Yes, stop fussing about the boy, Kate. Your fears are communicated to him and only make matters worse.'

'I don't fuss . . .' Kate began indignantly.

Harold Anatole was smiling. 'All women fuss — that is why they are so loved.' He looked at Simon. 'You wish to see the weekly reports?'

He fetched a chair for Kate and she sat down. Mike's head was dutifully bent over his exercise book, but he glanced up quickly and gave Kate a brief smile.

Simon had pulled up a chair and was straddled across it, his lean face grave as he read the handful of papers in his hand.

Mr. Anatole came to stand by Kate, bending down to speak softly in her ear.

'You see! Mr. Ellison takes an interest in the smallest thing. It is very good to work with such a person. His great-aunt believed in self-expression, so I teach the children to work. Mike, he asks questions all the time, but now I make him find the answers.' Mr. Anatole's deep laugh rang out, and Kate saw how all the children looked up and smiled at him.

Driving home with Simon, Kate said how much she liked Mr. Anatole. Simon gave her a quick, amused glance.

'I thought you would. That's why I took you. Now you can stop worrying about Mike's progress.'

'I wasn't worrying . . .' Kate began, but stopped as Simon smiled. 'Yes, I was, a little,' she said honestly. 'But I won't now.'

'Good.' Simon leaned back in the car, folding his arms and staring ahead. 'You know, Kate, sometimes people bite off more than they can chew. You did — without choice and without knowing it. Already you look a different girl. Prettier, more relaxed, less of a stern school-marm.'

Kate's cheeks flamed with indignant anger. 'It wasn't my fault —'

'I never said it was.'

'And besides, you only saw me when I was very tired or ill.'

'Which you were, most of the time, and undoubtedly your family suffered as a result. Kate, relax. Mike is growing fast, making his own friends here. Nancy is on top of the world. Now just forget them and enjoy yourself.'

She bit her lower lip quickly as she stifled the angry words she wanted to say. Why must he always criticize her?

'I am,' she said stiffly.

The car stopped outside the big house and Simon opened the door for her. 'Good,' he said curtly.

Kate got out and walked into the house, hearing the car drive away with Simon and Taro in it. She went upstairs to her bedroom and stood for a long thoughtful moment before the looking glass.

Simon had said she looked more relaxed. 'Prettier!' But it had been a statement of fact and not a compliment. Was she prettier? she wondered, as she stared at herself. Certainly she had put on weight, her cheeks were plumper and sun-tanned, her hair shining. She also looked much less tired, but then how could she be tired when she had nothing to do?

The days passed swiftly and at last the week came to an end. Kate realized that the rest against which she had helplessly rebelled had been good for her. She had grown to accept being waited on, having no work to do. Had learned to realize that Mike only needed her for a goodnight kiss or when he had something exciting to tell her. Now he would go off with his young friends, clasping bamboo poles as they went to spear shrimps. These, as cooked by Fetia, were delicious.

The evenings were the most difficult for Kate, for she realized that, because of her first week of illness, she was outside the 'circle'. Ian and Nancy danced or played table-tennis or merely teased one another idly during the hot evenings. Simon and Jerome would be talking 'shop' and Kate would sit there, feeling out of things, unable to join in the conversation, indeed believing that she would only be interrupting them if she tried to do so, so she had acquired the habit of going to bed early and reading in bed. Adam rarely stayed for the evening, only having dinner with them, and then vanishing. But at last the week was over, and on Sunday evening as Caterina said goodnight to them and Simon said he would drive her back to the hospital, she smiled at Kate.

'Now you can work as hard as you like,' she said.

'She may wish she couldn't when she sees what Adam's got lined up for her,' Simon said.

Caterina laughed. 'I'm sure Kate can cope!'

'I'm sure she can,' Simon said dryly. 'I'm equally sure she'll love it.'

Kate stood very still after they had gone. Now what had Simon meant by that? Did he still believe her to be a 'happy martyr'? Would she never be able to forget those words of his?

CHAPTER SEVEN

Simon took Kate to Adam's office which consisted of a large cool hut made of coconut logs. The windows were wide and there was no glass but there were heavy shutters in case the wind and rain grew too fierce, and there was a thatched roof.

Adam jumped up from his desk to welcome her. The broad-shouldered man with the dark hair and serious face was always friendly and Kate wondered what it would be like to work for him. At least, she thought gratefully, he would be patient if she made mistakes. He was not like Simon — a man who, according to Caterina, did not suffer fools gladly!

'Well, Adam,' Simon was saying cheerfully, 'here's your slave. I only hope she's half as useful to you as her sister is to me.' He turned to look at Kate briefly. 'Now you'll be happy.'

Left alone with Adam, Kate looked round

her. She had a large desk, a very modern typewriter, a huge file by her side. Adam started to explain the work he was doing and her interest was soon caught.

It was hard work but interesting, too. There were records to check, old accounts to reconcile. Great-Aunt Adèle had been a businesslike woman, but also extremely generous, and she had allowed many of the debts due to her to drag on indefinitely.

Soon Kate was able to write the letters needed — Adam would merely scribble on each letter in pencil what he wanted said and it was left to Kate to word the answer herself.

It was an ideal way of working, Kate decided. Breakfast in bed, a leisurely walk down to the office, a break for iced coffee at ten o'clock, and then a siesta from eleven o'clock to two o'clock every day and back to work until four o'clock. This, apparently, was the recognized routine on the island, and to Kate's surprise she found it made the work much easier. Tehutu would bring down a delicious cold lunch with salad which Adam and Kate would eat under the shade of the huge trees; afterwards they would lie in hammocks near the lagoon, sometimes talking, sometimes drowsy with the heat.

Kate found herself enjoying her work and the more she saw of Adam the more she liked him. Yet he was a strange man, rarely talking about himself.

One evening Kate, after dinner, had gone to Great-Aunt Adèle's room and was finishing one of the diaries that fascinated her. The door opened abruptly and Simon stood there, frowning.

'Why do you always vanish every evening, Kate?' he asked.

Kate was startled. 'Well, I . . . er . . .'

Simon closed the door behind him and came to straddle a chair near her.

'Don't you get on well with Adam?' he asked.

Kate coloured. 'Of course I get on well with him,' she said abruptly, 'but . . .'

'Well, he's sitting in there with no one to talk to. Nancy's playing table tennis with Ian as usual, and . . .'

'You and Jerome are talking shop,' Kate said sharply. 'As a rule Adam vanishes and I'm . . .'

'You're not interested in what you call "shop"?' Simon asked, his thick tufted eyebrows almost meeting. 'You find it boring, no doubt. Perhaps if you took the trouble to listen, you might learn something.'

Kate swallowed the quick angry reply. 'I — I always felt I might be in the way.'

'Oh, for . . .' Simon growled impatiently, and took a deep breath. He leaned forward. 'Kate, if there's one thing I cannot stand it's neurotic women who are afraid they might be in the way.' He stood up. 'I'd be glad if in future you would join us after dinner and we'll try to make the conversation general. Adam is out there, a very good sign, for I've been trying to include him in our circle without success. It must be your feminine influence that's thawing him.'

'I think Adam's shy. If he doesn't want to join us . . .' Kate began.

Simon swung round, his lean face grave. 'Has Adam talked about himself?'

'Very little,' Kate admitted. 'I know he's an orphan and, so he says, that he's completely lacking in ambition, and content to drift.'

Simon sat down again abruptly. 'That's a bare skeleton. Adam is an orphan, but he is a highly skilled accountant and had a very successful career. He was engaged to a lovely girl who walked out on him the morning of their wedding. That was bad enough, but the girl died on her honeymoon — both she and her husband were killed in a car crash. Her husband happened to be

Adam's best friend. Adam just went to pieces. I've known him for years, and when I decided to do this —' he waved his hand vaguely — 'I asked Adam to help me. It was a battle. He had crawled into a little hole and wanted to stay there. I wouldn't let him. I made him see I needed him. That's as far as I've got. Night after night, he goes to his room and mopes . . .' Simon paused.

Meeting Simon's thoughtful eyes, Kate was conscious of her surprise at his reaction to Adam's unhappiness. She would have expected Simon to see it as weakness, but instead he viewed it sympathetically. Could it be that Caterina was right — and Simon had also lost the girl he loved? Surely, Kate thought, that could be the only explanation for Simon's sympathy with Adam.

'Somehow we've got to bring Adam back to life,' Simon went on gravely. 'I think you can help, Kate.'

'Me?' said Kate, startled.

Simon nodded. 'Yes, you, Kate. You're a quiet sensible sort of girl, friendly, easy to talk to. Nancy's far too young. Besides, she's wrapped up — as they say — in Ian, though what she can see in the boy, I don't know.'

Again Kate noticed the hint of hardness and dislike in Simon's voice that she had noticed before when he spoke of his nephew.

Simon stood up. 'Can I count on your help, then, Kate?'

Kate closed the diary and put it away in the drawer.

'Of course, Simon,' she said. 'But I don't know what I can do.'

'Don't try to do anything or you'll fail dismally,' Simon said crisply. 'Just be yourself. You must have some interest or hobby you can talk about . . . apart from knitting sweaters for the family,' he added.

'I . . . I used to collect stamps,' Kate said slowly.

Simon's tufted eyebrows lifted quizzically. 'Well, well, well! A little philatelist. Now that's a fortunate thing, Kate. Just one moment . . .' He bent down and opened the bottom drawer. 'Great-Aunt Adèle was also a philatelist. Maybe you'd like to look at this.'

Kate turned the pages of the book slowly. There were many early stamps she had never seen. She lifted her face to look at the tall man by her side and her eyes were bright with interest.

'Thanks awfully. I'd love to look through it.'

'Bring it along to the drawing room, then,' said Simon. 'It might be the opening gambit you're looking for with Adam.'

How right Simon had been, Kate thought, later that night as she lay in bed. Adam had helped her put the heavy book on a table, had sat by her side as she turned the pages, discussing the stamps and discovering that they were both interested.

Kate stretched and yawned and half-closed her eyes, completely shutting out all thought of Adam as she remembered Simon's words. They had not been very complimentary, had they? she thought. What was it he had said?

'You're a quiet sensible sort of girl. Friendly, easy to talk to.'

Kate pulled a wry face. Somehow she could not imagine anyone describing Caterina in such prosaic words. Was that how Simon saw her? It was not a pleasant thought, somehow.

There was a sudden tap on the bedroom door and it opened. Nancy stood there, her loose yellow cotton dressing-gown barely hiding her blue shortie pyjamas.

'Kate, have you heard the news?' she began, her young, pretty face tragic.

Kate's heart seemed to skip a beat. 'Simon?'

'No — Ian, of course,' said Nancy, coming into the room to curl up at the foot of Kate's bed. Nancy's face was miserable, the corners of her mouth drooping.

'Is Ian ill?' Kate asked.

'Of course he isn't ill,' Nancy said irritably. 'He was there at dinner, but he only told me tonight that he's leaving next week.'

'Leaving?'

Nancy nodded, her honey-gold hair tied back in a pony tail swinging. 'I couldn't believe it when he told me. I thought he was here for good. What will I do, Kate?' she asked, her voice tragic. 'Without Ian, I'll be bored to tears!'

It might have been funny if it hadn't been, as Kate knew, tragic to Nancy. Nancy was the sort of girl who needed companionship, to belong to lots of clubs and always be out. She rarely read a book, only dipping into magazines, and soon got bored. Kate knew a moment of dismay. Everything was going so smoothly — now if Nancy got bored and unhappy, it might spoil things for Jerome.

'We'll think of something,' Kate said soothingly, just as she had said for many years. Nancy had never been an easy child, easily dissatisfied and discontented.

'There's Simon and . . .'

'He and Jerome never stop talking shop,' Nancy sighed miserably, putting into words Kate's own thoughts.

'Maybe we can find a way to cure them,'

Kate said brightly. 'What about bridge?'

'You know I hate the game,' Nancy said cuttingly, but Kate saw that Nancy was cheering up. 'We could play scrabble,' Nancy added thoughtfully.

'There's me and Adam,' Kate reminded her.

'Adam . . .' Nancy said slowly. 'He's an odd character, Kate. What d'you make of him? I can never get more than two words out at a time.' She gave Kate a quick sharp look. 'You seemed to be getting on very well tonight, I must say. What was the magic word you used?'

It took Kate quite a few moments to understand what Nancy meant, but when she did, she laughed.

'Stamps,' she said.

Nancy slid to her feet and yawned. 'I'm afraid I know nothing about stamps.'

'When's Ian going?' Kate asked.

'I told you,' Nancy said crossly. 'Next week. He's going back to his mother. She misses him, he says. Actually I think he was at some university and got sent down and was sent out here to his uncle in disgrace and now, he says, his mother's got lonely, so she's decided to forgive him. He's kind of soppy, Kate. A real mother's boy,' she finished scornfully.

'I thought you liked him,' Kate said, abruptly.

Nancy shrugged. 'He was all right. After all, he's the only man on the island who talked to me, so he was better than nothing.'

She walked out of the room, slamming the door behind her. Kate lay very still. Poor Nancy! She had probably thought herself in love with Ian and imagined he adored her, and now she was waking up to the truth. Ian had just been killing time! Whenever Nancy spoke slightingly of people, it invariably meant that she liked them more than was wise.

Kate snuggled down between the sheets. Maybe it was a blessing in disguise. Simon had said Nancy was too young to help Adam, but perhaps if they started playing cards and had social sorts of evenings, that would help Adam. At any rate, it was a good idea, and if Nancy needed any encouragement, Kate knew that she would help her. If Simon objected to his evenings of talking 'shop' being interrupted, Kate could always tell him that it was to help Adam. Simon could hardly take offence at that!

Simon was a strange man in many ways. No patience with his nephew who might have been a little wild and foolish — but who wasn't like that in his teens? Yet Simon had every sympathy with Adam who had lost the girl he loved. Kate felt more sure than ever that somewhere in his past, Simon had been hurt by a girl, incredible as it seemed. Maybe Simon had been a different person before — a nicer person, perhaps.

Chapter Eight

Caterina had dined with them and was sitting on the couch in the drawing-room after dinner, elegant and beautiful in a straight white silk frock. Kate, curled up in an armchair, talking to Adam, with his slow thoughtful speech, and Nancy, with her quick laugh and jokes, found herself glancing at Caterina constantly.

How very lovely she was, Kate thought. That ash-blonde hair, twisted now into a neat roll on top of her head, her straight dark brows emphasizing the smouldering look in her surprisingly dark eyes. What colour were they? Kate wondered for the hundredth time. When Caterina was being a doctor, very brisk and authoritative, her eyes looked dark blue. When she was warm and friendly, they looked violet.

Kate looked down at her own amber-coloured silk frock with distaste. How homely it seemed. Or was it simply that everything Caterina wore immediately became elegant?

Adam laughed suddenly and, startled, for he rarely laughed, Kate turned to look at him. Nancy's eyes were shining as she teased him.

'And you didn't know it, Adam,' she said, laughing as she accused him. 'Where were you dragged up?'

'In the gutter,' he joked back, his normally grave face momentarily bright with amusement.

Kate's gaze passed on to Simon. He was sitting back in his deep armchair, his arms folded, his eyes half closed as if he was thinking, his lean face stern. Had something angered him? It was impossible to connect a man like Simon — strong, decisive, sometimes hard — with a word like 'sulking', yet Kate found herself thinking of the word. Had he and Caterina quarrelled? she wondered.

Normally when Caterina dined with them, they spent the hours afterwards talking. But tonight Caterina and Simon seemed to have nothing to say to one another.

Kate moved a little restlessly. She was eager to go up to Mike's room and see if he was asleep, but she hesitated, for she knew it would only give Simon a chance to accuse her of 'fussing'. A few days before, Mike had badly scraped his feet on the coral reef. Simon had taken him to the hospital and Caterina had treated the deep scratches, but they were not healing quickly, and although Caterina treated the matter lightly, Mike had been sent to bed, and Kate had thought he looked feverish.

Ever since Simon had spoken to Kate about Adam, Kate had made a point of sitting in the drawing-room after dinner. Now Ian had gone, Nancy joined them and usually they all played scrabble or some guessing game, but when Caterina came, they always put away such childish things — those were Simon's own words, Kate found herself thinking — and had adult conversation! But tonight something was very wrong. Kate could sense the tension in the air.

Simon stood up abruptly, asking them to excuse him as he had a letter to write. No one except Kate seemed to notice he had gone. Nancy was trying to teach Adam a rhyme she had learned as a child. She was laughing because he was pretending he could not remember a word, and Kate thought, remembering Simon's unexpected anxiety about Adam, that Simon must be feeling pleased about it. Not that Simon would ever say anything. He seemed to find it hard to give praise, even when it was due. Yet, oddly enough, Nancy loved working for him. Nancy, Kate thought, who normally needed appreciation and spoken praise.

Caterina and Jerome were involved in an argument about the new hospital that would have to be built to take care of any ill or injured tourists and the large staff required to run the different hotels. Jerome had produced a massive drawing which Caterina was studying.

Quietly Kate stood up and left the room, hurrying a little as she reached the staircase, her honey-brown silky hair bobbing as she moved. This was her chance to slip in and see Mike.

He was sound asleep, his thin body sprawled across the bed under the mosquito netting. Gently Kate straightened his limbs, tucked the white sheet loosely round him, and brushed his forehead with her fingers. He seemed cooler. Maybe the injection Caterina had given him was helping.

She left the room, closing the door quietly behind her, just as Jerome came along the passage.

He smiled. 'Two minds with the same thought,' he said quietly. 'How is he?'

'He seems much cooler,' said Kate, grateful that it was Jerome who had seen her leaving Mike's room, and not Simon.

Jerome nodded. 'Caterina said these things take time. Now I'm beginning to understand Simon's insistence that we all wear sneakers when we're on the reef. Caterina says the cuts can be very dangerous.' He paused, looking shrewdly at Kate. 'You're not really worried about Mike, are you?' he added.

Kate shook her head. 'Not worried at all, Jerome, it's just I thought he might be thirsty or . . . or maybe couldn't sleep.'

Jerome's hand was warm on Kate's bare arm. 'Dear Kate, I often wonder how we'd have managed without you,' he said, his voice a little unsteady. 'The illness you've nursed us through, the depressions . . .'

'I loved it, Jerome,' Kate said quickly, and realized that it was the truth.

She had loved it. Loved being needed by them, being necessary to them, in fact. Maybe that was the reason for her feeling of being out of things here. No one needed her. And a woman, Kate thought worriedly, had to be 'needed' if she was to feel complete. Maybe Simon understood that — maybe he hadn't meant to be sarcastic when he called her 'a happy martyr', for that was what she had been! Yet his voice had been so . . . so chilling, so unpleasant.

'Kate, we're very lucky to have a doctor like Caterina here,' Jerome was saying earnestly.

They walked down the passage to an alcove where there was a couch by a large window. It was uncurtained and they could see a huge orange moon in the dark sky.

'I know we are,' agreed Kate.

They sat down, Kate tucking her feet under her frock. It was not often she and Jerome were alone and she welcomed the little moment of intimacy. She was very fond of Jerome and realized how much she had missed his companionship.

'She's a wonderful woman,' Jerome went on thoughtfully. 'I know she lost the man she loved, but I can't understand why she's never married again.'

'I agree,' Kate agreed quickly. 'She's so lovely to look at, and so intelligent.'

'And such a fine woman,' Jerome added. He hesitated for a moment, stroking the pattern of the damask that covered the couch as if he was seeking the right words. 'D'you think Simon and Caterina are in love?' he asked abruptly.

Kate had asked herself the same question a hundred times but having it put into blunt words came, surprisingly, as a shock.

'I . . . I don't know,' she said slowly.

'Sometimes I think they are, sometimes I wonder. The way Caterina talks about Simon makes me think she is.'

'The trouble, to my mind, is that Caterina is a strong woman,' Jerome pointed out. 'Maybe Simon is looking for a doormat.'

They both laughed.

'You could be right,' Kate said. 'He's so sure of himself, maybe it irritates him to have anyone stand up to him.'

'On the other hand,' said Jerome, 'it might be good for him.'

Kate laughed. 'I wish I could do it, but I do so hate it when he gets sarcastic,' she confessed.

Jerome looked startled. 'I don't think he means to be. It's just his sense of humour.'

'A very strange one,' Kate said dryly.

Jerome looked worried. 'Kate, he's a kind man. He wouldn't willingly hurt anyone.'

'I know, but . . .' Kate agreed. They sat in silence for a moment, Kate telling herself that perhaps she had been foolish to let Simon browbeat her. Maybe she should stand up to him.

Jerome turned abruptly. 'Kate, I've just thought of something. D'you think it's her work? Caterina's, I mean? After all, she's a dedicated doctor and she loves her work here. How would that affect her life with Simon, I wonder?'

Startled, Kate swung round to look at him. 'But she couldn't just stop being a doctor.'

'That's what I mean.'

For a moment, they stared at one another and then Jerome went on:

'You see, Kate, this isn't the beginning and end of Simon's life. He's a wealthy, ambitious man, his head's full of new projects. That means he'll be travelling. How does that fit in with Caterina's long-term plans for this island?'

'Perhaps he could make this his headquarters?'

Jerome looked sceptical. 'What sort of marriage would that be? Can you see Simon accepting a part-time wife?'

Kate found herself smiling. 'No, I certainly can't. But if Caterina loves him . . .'

'Ah, but does she love him that much? Caterina is a woman, not a girl on the threshold of life. She's chosen her path, I doubt if she'd ever leave it,' Jerome said thoughtfully. 'What a terrible choice to be asked to make . . .' He stopped speaking abruptly as Nancy came up the stairs.

'Hi!' she greeted them cheerfully. 'Having a natter?' She came to join them. 'Party's broken up. Simon, looking very stern, came in after you two vanished and suggested Adam and I played table tennis. You should have seen poor Adam's face!' She laughed. 'I don't think he's ever played in his life, and he got in such a mess trying to get out of playing that I took pity on him and said I was tired.'

Kate stood up. 'I am,' she confessed, yawning. ' 'Night, you two.'

' 'Night,' they both said, with one voice, and Kate left them, Nancy curling up on the couch by her stepfather's side as they began to talk.

Alone in her room, the huge golden-red moon shining in, Kate quickly undressed in the dark, tying her soft green dressing-gown round her, thrusting her feet into matching mules. She went to the window, staring out at the magical beauty of the scene — the palms starkly still in the moonlight, the wide silver pathway across the dark lagoon. Distantly she could hear music, the twanging of guitars, the soft nostalgic music of the Polynesians.

On an impulse, she opened the windows and stepped out on to the balcony, quickly closing the screen doors behind her to keep the mosquitoes out of her room. She stood very still, drinking in the beauty before her. Where else in the world could you see, hear and smell such beauty? The strange sweet tang of the tropical flowers drifted up towards her — the odd nocturnal sounds of birds and animals, the distant roar of the breakers on the reef and all the time, the quiet but stirring music of the singers.

'Look, we've been over this a thousand times,' a deep voice said from below.

Startled, Kate leant over the balcony rail and then drew back hastily into the shadow thrown by the over-hanging roof. Her bedroom was above the drawing-room and Simon and Caterina must have just walked out into the garden. Kate stood very still. What should she do? Discreetly cough to let them know they were not alone? Or would Simon think she had been snooping? Open the door which they were bound to hear and which would be even worse? Before she had time to decide, it was too late, so she stood still, flattening herself against the wall.

'And likely to go over it a thousand times more,' Caterina replied, her voice husky yet trembling with what sounded like anger.

'Caterina, please be sensible. See it from my point of view,' said Simon, his voice almost pleading.

'You want me to be sensible?' Caterina's voice rose slightly. 'How like a man! You are all the same. Impossible!' Her slight accent was becoming stronger as if she was growing angrier every moment. 'Selfish. What about me? I am a dedicated woman and you talk such nonsense. It has happened before — always you men say . . .'

'Caterina,' Simon's voice was stern, 'I wouldn't argue that, for I do respect your point of view. At the same time, you must see that it's ridiculous to expect me to agree . . .'

'Simon —' Caterina's husky voice broke, 'I refuse to argue. Why I have patience with you, I do not know!'

'I do,' Simon replied dryly. 'You have a one-track mind and refuse to see my point of view.'

'You've a one-track mind, you mean. Selfish, blind, unable to look ahead. What sort of future will . . .'

'Look, let's stop arguing and call it a night,' Simon said abruptly. 'My answer is still no — I cannot agree.'

'That is your last word? It is senseless to argue with so stubborn a man,' Caterina told him. 'I do not wish to stay any longer. My car is in the drive. I will go!'

'I'll follow in my car in case . . .' Simon began, but Caterina cut him short abruptly.

'Please do not trouble. You will only offend me more. I feel exhausted enough already without driving to the hospital with your bright lights continually chivvying me to drive faster.'

'As you wish,' Simon said stiffly, and Kate heard him moving and then the closing of the french windows below.

She could see Caterina hurrying across the velvet smooth lawn in her high heels. And Kate saw something else, something that was most disturbing.

Caterina was crying.

Slapping the mosquitoes that had been viciously biting her, Kate hurried into her bedroom, sliding into bed, pulling the sheet over her. Why had Caterina wept? What was the quarrel about? Perhaps Jerome was right — Caterina and Simon were in love, but neither would give way. Caterina would always want to be a doctor — yet wasn't it natural for Simon to want, as Jerome put it, a full-time wife?

CHAPTER NINE

The next day Simon left the island. Adam told Kate that Simon had business to attend to in Papeete and might be away for a week or longer, but Kate wondered if it had anything to do with Simon's quarrel with Caterina.

It was a strange week to Kate — somehow the island seemed different. The sun still shone, the strange wind still blew the palm trees wildly in abandoned dances — the islanders still sang and strummed their guitars, but the island was different.

Maybe it was the relaxed atmosphere, Kate decided. Adam and Nancy seemed to be becoming more friendly, Jerome spent several evenings at the hospital with Caterina, and Kate found herself free to sit in Great-Aunt Adèle's studio, gazing at the paintings or reading the diaries.

The day Simon returned on a schooner was one Kate would never forget. She was

working with Adam in the office when Tehutu, the Polynesian maid, came running.
The pretty girl looked terrified. Kate was
wanted.

'Quick, quick, quick!' called Tehutu, and
turned and ran back to the big house.

Kate and Adam stared at one another.

'I didn't know Simon was back,' said
Adam.

'Why does he want to see me so urgently?'
Kate asked, absurdly scared.

'Probably some small thing,' Adam said
comfortingly. 'Simon's living under great
tension and the smallest problem can ex-
plode into a major disaster.'

'That doesn't sound like him,' Kate said.

Adam smiled. 'I know, but even Simon is
human — at times. You'd better hurry, Kate,
don't make it worse.'

Kate obeyed, telling herself it was ridiculous to feel so scared. Simon was only a
man, after all. The worst that could happen
would be for him to be displeased with her
work and say she must go — and he
wouldn't do that, for he was pleased with
both Nancy's and Jerome's!

Simon was alone in his office when Kate
reached it. There was no sign of Nancy,
Kate noticed, but then that was probably
because no one had known Simon was

returning that day and Nancy had no work left to do.

'You wanted to see me?' Kate asked as she stood in the doorway, Simon ignoring her while he finished writing some letters.

He looked up. 'Yes,' he said curtly. 'Sit down.'

Kate obeyed, annoyed with herself for feeling like a schoolgirl in the presence of the headmaster.

Simon looked at her, his strange grey-gold eyes narrowed thoughtfully. It seemed an endless moment. Was he doing it on purpose, Kate wondered, to terrify her? Defiantly she lifted her head and looked at him. When he spoke, his accusing voice and unexpected words were like a slap in the face.

'Why did you tell Georgia that Jerome only got the job because I liked you?' he asked.

Kate caught her breath. She was on her feet in a moment.

'I never said anything of the sort,' she began angrily — and then stopped speaking, feeling the hot colour in her cheeks.

Simon looked up at her. 'You can't deny it, can you?' he said coldly.

'Yes, I can,' retorted Kate, finding courage again. 'I didn't tell her that, but she asked me how well I knew you and I told the truth. That I had only seen you three times. The first was when I went to see you before Jerome got the job and . . .'

'Which implied that it was because of you I gave Jerome the job,' Simon pointed out.

Kate coloured again. 'I didn't mean it to sound that way, because it wasn't the truth.'

'It most certainly wasn't,' Simon said with cutting contempt. 'I've never yet engaged a man because I liked his daughter — or stepdaughter. In fact, had I met you first, I doubt very much if I'd have considered Jerome at all. I dislike men who are tied down by domestic ties.'

'Jerome was not tied down,' Kate began.

'I engaged Jerome because I believed him to be a good architect,' Simon continued, ignoring Kate's words. 'I offered him the job and discovered that he was in bondage to his family.'

'That's not true and you know it,' Kate said angrily. 'Jerome was never in bondage, as you put it. But a married man — and a father — has certain responsibilities and . . .'

'How smug you sound, Kate,' Simon said. 'Is life as straightforward as that? A man marries and so he must never again do what he wants to do? He must knuckle under and do what his family says?'

151

Kate was so angry she could hardly speak. 'You're deliberately distorting everything, and you know it! Jerome was never in bondage to us. I tried to keep the home together . . . if I'd been older, able to earn more money, we might have managed, but . . .' Suddenly her anger vanished as she remembered something. 'Are people talking about us in Papeete?' she asked.

Simon nodded. 'Yes, they are.'

'Then it's your fault,' she said accusingly, her voice triumphant. 'Everyone saw us when you carried me down the pier in your arms, like some bold sheikh kidnapping a slave!' she added scornfully. 'No wonder people are talking when you do things like that!'

She saw by Simon's face that her taunt had reached its mark. He had forgotten that ridiculous moment on the pier.

'I was in a hurry and you were walking slowly,' Simon began, and then stopped as if recognizing the foolishness of such an excuse.

Kate was still caught up in her courage-giving anger. 'I think you owe me an apology,' she told him. 'I certainly don't want my name linked with yours!'

She was startled and annoyed, when Simon burst out laughing. She stood there, staring at him indignantly, as he laughed and laughed, moving in his chair as if unable to stop laughing.

'I don't think it's very funny,' she said stiffly.

In a moment, Simon stopped laughing. He stood up and came to stand near her, towering above her. Then he put his hands on her shoulders and she could feel the pressure of his warm fingers.

'It isn't really funny, Kate,' he admitted, 'but I was furious with you for having got me mixed up in the irritating gossip that Papeete is full of — and then I learn it was my own fault. I apologize,' he said solemnly, but there was laughter still in his eyes.

Kate found herself smiling up at him. 'I apologize, too,' she said. 'Maybe I should have made sure Georgia understood what I meant, but she was always in such a hurry.'

'I know,' said Simon, and took his hands from her shoulders. 'Well now, having cleared the air, where's that lazy sister of yours?'

'We didn't expect you back yet and she's finished all you left her to do,' Kate said quickly.

Simon frowned. 'Do stop clucking like a broody hen, Kate, I'm not going to tear a strip off Nancy. I just have some letters to dictate. She's probably swimming or sun-bathing. I'll find her.'

Kate walked slowly back through the hot sunshine to the office. She felt absurdly elated and ridiculously deflated at the same moment. Elated because she'd had the courage to stand up to Simon — deflated because it had seemed an anti-climax when he scolded her for fussing. Had she leapt to Nancy's defence? Was she too inclined to worry about the others? Yet she couldn't help it. She loved them. She was made that way.

Adam looked up with a grin. 'Glad to see you're in one piece,' he said.

Kate sat down. 'Just a misunderstanding,' she said tersely. 'For once Simon was wrong and apologized.'

Adam whistled softly. 'He actually apologized?'

Kate turned round and suddenly began to laugh. 'It was funny, really, Adam,' she confessed. 'I couldn't see it before, but . . .'

Adam nodded. 'I know.' He glanced at his watch. 'Time for a tea break,' he said cheerfully. 'I guess you can do with some.'

Kate nodded. 'As Ian would have said, you can say that again.'

'Talking of Ian,' said Adam as they sipped

the hot sweet tea, 'Nancy must miss him a lot.'

'She must,' Kate agreed, 'but she's never said so.'

Adam looked thoughtful as he stirred his tea. 'She wasn't in love with him?'

'In love?' Kate was startled. 'Oh no. She's had sort of crushes, you know, but I don't think she's ever been in love.'

'She's very young,' Adam said, still thoughtful.

'Very young,' Kate agreed. 'Far too young to know her own mind,' she added. 'I think she found Ian good fun and he was her own age which she liked . . .'

Adam put down his cup with a little bang and stood up. 'Yes, she must have liked it,' he said, his voice strange for a moment. 'Back to the grindstone, Kate.'

Kate swallowed the last of the tea. 'Yes, back to the grindstone,' she agreed with a rueful smile. 'It seems a crime to have to work on a day like this.'

Adam was already bent over his ledgers. 'Yes, it does,' he said briefly, as if annoyed about something. Kate looked at him, gave a little helpless shrug and got down to work. It looked as if Adam, as well as Simon, had 'moods', after all.

That evening, Simon was in fine spirits

and after dinner they played scrabble with zest, but Kate noticed that Adam was very quiet and Nancy asked Kate before they went to bed what was biting Adam.

'He was just getting friendly,' Nancy said, and Kate was startled at the wistful note in her voice. 'Why has he changed tonight?'

Kate said she didn't know. 'He was a bit moody today,' she added. 'Probably he'll be over it tomorrow.'

'Let's hope so,' Nancy said fervently. 'We're so cooped up here and there are so few of us that we've simply got to be good friends.'

Kate was startled, and yet, when she came to think of it, Nancy was right. They simply had to be good friends. Well, at least, Kate thought gratefully, Simon seemed to have forgiven her little outburst of anger and her refusal to be accused by him of something she had not done, for he had been his usual self that night.

The next day, with unexpected suddenness, the weather changed. A high wind screamed its way through the island, twisting and bending the palm trees, sending tropical rain pounding against the windows and beating on the roof, cutting out the view with a dismal cloud of grey water. Mike's feet took a turn for the worse and he was back in bed, Adam's 'office' which was really a coconut-log hut, leaked shockingly and work in it came temporarily to a stand-still.

'It won't hurt you to have a few days' holiday,' Simon said crisply to Kate after Adam had said it wasn't worth risking the ledgers and books getting wet on their way to the big house, so he had locked everything away in the steel cupboards. 'You can do some serious work on the diaries, Kate,' he went on. 'It seems to me that what my great-aunt has recorded is worth publishing. What do you feel about it?'

Kate looked up at him. 'I agree,' she told him. 'If I find them fascinating to read — not only the human element but all the background about life here in those days — many people would and it would surely be a help to anyone wanting to settle on an island,' she added with a little smile, remembering some of Great-Aunt Adèle's problems before she got the islanders really organized.

'Good. Well, Kate, I'd be grateful if you'd sketch out some vague idea of compiling them into a book. Then we'll get a draft typed out and I'll send it along to a publisher I know rather well. If he's interested, I'll get hold of some writer who could make it into a book. Right?'

'Of course,' said Kate.

So while the rain beat dismally against the windows and the wind went screeching round like an irritable banshee, Kate sat in the annexe, reading the yellowed pages of the diaries, making notes, trying to work out which portions of the books would be most interesting to the average reader. Kate herself was most interested in the diaries written in the early days when Adèle Scott was fighting her heartache and loneliness and the bitterness against her family that she could not overcome. But perhaps the average reader would not be . . .

The door opened suddenly and Kate recognized Simon's firm footstep.

'How's it going, Kate?' he asked.

He must have just come in from the rain, Kate thought, for his short fair hair was wet and his lean face had rain still trickling down it. His khaki shorts and shirt were rumpled as if he'd been wearing one of the big mackintosh capes they wore in wet weather. Now he was shaking his head, the small cold raindrops flying towards Kate.

'I'm just wondering if the part about her husband is too personal and too sad,' she told him.

Simon lifted a chair in one hand, swung it

round and straddled it. He looked at her gravely.

'Too personal? I don't know what you mean.'

Kate coloured. 'Well, if you lost someone you loved very much, would you want your . . . your anguish and your tears read about by lots of strangers?' she asked.

Simon frowned. 'Frankly, I've never thought of it. Do you feel she gives a solution? I mean, what she writes, would it help anyone to get over such a loss?'

Kate felt uncomfortable. Were they on dangerous ground? Caterina had said that Simon had once been badly hurt by a woman.

'Yes,' she said slowly, 'I do think it could help.'

'You've read about the rainbow shell?' he asked.

Kate nodded. 'Yes, she says that when the burden of her sorrow grew too great, she would take out the rainbow shell and . . .'

Simon was not listening. He stood up, strode with his usual long effortless strides to the cupboard which he opened. In a moment he turned round, carrying something very carefully in his hands.

'This is the rainbow shell,' he said.

Kate looked at the shell. It was not very

big nor even a very unusual shape, but what made it different from any other shell was the colours. Now she could see why Mrs. Scott had called it the rainbow shell, for it was veined with palest pink, a turquoise blue, a faint yellow and pale green specks. All the colours of the rainbow.

Simon put it carefully on the desk and straddled the chair again.

'Have you come to the part in the diaries where she explains how she was given the rainbow shell?'

'No . . . no, I haven't,' Kate confessed. The diaries were thick books with close lines filled with meticulously neat but small handwriting, and often she had caught herself skipping some of the more pedantic phrases. She preferred the parts where old Mrs. Scott — who had been young Mrs. Scott when she wrote the diaries — had been completely uninhibited and had written in natural phrases about her loneliness and pain.

Simon rested his arms on the back of the chair, his lean face thoughtful.

'Her husband gave it to her soon after they reached Papeete, before he was ill. In one of the diaries, she quotes a poem.

' "My heart is like a singing bird

Whose nest is in a water'd shoot,
My heart is like an apple tree
Whose boughs are bent with thick-set
    fruit . . .
My heart is like a rainbow shell
That paddles in a halcyon sea;
My heart is gladder than all these.
Because my love is come to me . . ." '

Simon paused, his deep voice coming to a standstill. Kate sat very still. She would never have believed that Simon could show so much emotion. He had recited the poem beautifully and she felt goose pimples on her skin as a result. But what he said next surprised her still more.

'If only Great-Aunt Adèle had known how lucky she was,' Simon said slowly. 'Even though she had her love for so short a time, at least she knew that he loved her . . .'

There was another silence, even more awkward, for Kate felt she should say something yet had no idea what was the right thing to say. How wistful Simon had sounded.

And then his mood changed. He was on his feet, picking up the shell gently and smiling at Kate.

'I bet that gave you a shock, Kate,' he said.

'I'm sure you didn't think I could quote poetry.'

'No, I didn't,' Kate admitted honestly. 'Who wrote it?'

He shrugged. 'Rossetti, I think, but I'm not sure. Would it also surprise you to learn that once upon a time when I was young, I also wrote poetry?' He was smiling as he looked down at her, and Kate smiled back.

'Nothing would surprise me about you, Simon,' she said.

Momentarily he looked startled and then he laughed, turning to put the shell away, coming back to stand by Kate.

'I suppose I'm a sentimental fool to keep it, but . . .'

'You couldn't throw it away,' Kate cried, shocked.

'What shall I do with it, then?'

'Give it to your children one day,' she suggested.

'I'm not interested in love. I told you that,' he said. Kate saw that he was teasing her, so she smiled.

'Every man has his Achilles' heel . . .' she began.

Simon laughed. 'I bet Georgia Appleby said that. Right? I knew it was. Kate, when I first came to Papeete, there was quite a stampede. The single girls thought it was time I got married, the older women tried to matchmake. In the end, even Georgia gave up, but I know that she won't be happy until I'm marched to the altar. Why is every man supposed to get married?'

'You think love is stupid?' Kate asked.

Simon leant forward and put his hand on hers. It was a strong hand, a warm hand, but also a gentle hand.

'Kate, I do believe in love, but I think it happens very rarely. And it's even more rare for both parties to love sincerely. Usually one of them gets hurt.'

He lifted his hand from hers and walked to the window, looking at the wild scene outside, where the palm trees were being swayed and pummelled by the wind and rain. He spoke over his shoulder.

'Kate, my parents stayed together for the sake of us children. I think it was the biggest mistake they ever made, for we grew up in an atmosphere which was either one of bickering, long frightening silences or sudden outbursts of furious anger. Two of my brothers rushed into marriage to escape this, and both were unhappy. Ian's mother was one of the wives. She and my brother Bill eloped when they were very young and they hated one another. I had known them when they were so crazily in love that they were prepared to be cut off without a penny — yet a few years later, they could hardly bear to speak to one another . . .'

Simon was walking backwards and forwards across the small room, hands clasped behind his back, face looking thinner than usual, the life gone from it, his mouth sad.

'Kate,' he went on, 'I'm not a cynic and I believe that some people continue to love one another. Unfortunately my own experience has usually been that one person either loves too much, too jealously and possessively, or not enough . . .'

He paused, and Kate, sitting very still, very conscious that this confidence was something she had never expected, said nothing, but wondered if Simon was thinking of Caterina. Did he feel she did not love him 'enough' because she could not give up her career? Though to Caterina, Kate thought, medicine was more than just a career — it was her life's work.

'What do you feel about love, Kate?' he asked abruptly.

Taken aback, Kate stared at him. 'Why, I . . . I hadn't thought . . .'

'You've never been in love?' Simon asked, looking surprised.

She shook her head. 'Never, but then . . . then I haven't known many men,' she added honestly. 'Mummy was happy with both her husbands, though sometimes she got worried about things, but I just took it for granted that if you love someone, it lasts.'

Simon smiled wryly. 'How blissful to be so young and innocent,' he said, glancing at his watch. 'I must be off. I told Jerome . . .'

In a moment he had gone and she was alone. She stared at the wild world outside. How strange it was that Simon should have talked like that to her!

That evening Caterina joined them. Simon had driven to fetch her, for the wind was very strong, almost approaching hurricane strength, he said, after they had both raced indoors, covered in heavy mackintosh capes, Caterina undid the scarf with which she had covered her head and her hair was immaculate, brushed back into a loose chignon. She was wearing black for once, a plain straight frock that seemed to bring out the highlights in her ash-blonde hair and make her skin look creamier than ever. She sat near Kate while Simon was preparing the drinks and smiled at her.

'Green suits you, Kate,' Caterina said gently. 'You're looking very happy tonight.'

Kate coloured. 'I am . . . feeling happy, I mean. I was reading the diaries this afternoon and . . .'

Caterina laughed and raised her hand. She glanced quickly at Simon, but he was too far away to hear what they were saying.

'You don't have to tell me, Kate,' she said, laughing.

'Simon recited a poem to you about the precious rainbow shell! Am I right?'

Kate felt her cheeks growing hot again. 'Yes, he did, but . . .'

'Oh, Kate, dear child,' Caterina said gently, 'I am sorry if I've hurt you. You were flattered because Simon confided in you. Is that it? And now I have blown the bubble apart, for it is obvious that you are not the first woman to whom he has recited the poem so movingly, so magnificently? I am sorry.'

'It's all right . . . there's nothing to be sorry about,' Kate stumbled, trying to find the right words, trying to hide the fact that she was disappointed to learn that Simon had confided in other people as well as herself. Yet what right had she to expect to be the only one? Simon had never shown any particular liking for her. In fact, quite the reverse, Kate thought miserably, wondering why she felt so upset. She felt the gentle touch of Caterina's hand on her arm.

'You must not look so upset, Kate, dear child. You may not be the only woman to whom he recites poetry, but it shows that he does consider you an adult. He would not speak thus to everyone — not to Nancy, for example,' she added, her voice kind.

'I'm not upset,' Kate said quickly, wondering how to change the subject, how to escape from Caterina's shrewd, amused eyes.

Jerome came into the room and Kate drew a sigh of relief.

'Caterina, you have braved the elements,' said Jerome, his voice jocular, as he came to join them.

'I am a woman of courage, Jerome,' Caterina told him laughingly, her slight accent suddenly pronounced.

Kate murmured something and slipped out of the room. Upstairs in the quiet safety of her bedroom, she gazed blindly at her reflection. Why had she felt so disappointed when she learned that Simon confided in everyone — or nearly everyone — the story of the rainbow shell? Why should she feel so deflated — so . . . so ridiculously miserable?

It could only be because she hated feeling on the outside of everything again; because she felt that Simon had, at last, accepted her — just as he had accepted Nancy from the beginning.

CHAPTER TEN

The squally gales and torrential rain died away as abruptly as they had started and the island was once more a land of sunshine, steam rising in great misty clouds from the rain-drenched earth. Once again the sound of guitars and singing filled the air, the deliciously haunting scent of tropical flowers teased their nostrils; and they could enjoy the beauty of the blue Pacific with its great white rollers and the placidity of the lagoons with the small boats with the fishermen in them.

A feast was to be held the next day, Simon had told them one night at dinner.

'This is to welcome me back from my week's visit to Papeete,' he said. 'They snatch at any excuse for a feast,' he added with a wry smile. 'It can be fascinating, Kate. I'll take you to see the preparations.'

Caterina laughed. 'What time have you, Simon?' she asked. 'You'll forget or be too busy. Let me initiate Kate into the mysteries of Polynesian feasts. I'll call for you in my car, Kate.'

'Thanks,' said Kate.

'What about you, Nancy?' Caterina asked, looking across the table.

'Nancy's got work to do,' Simon said at once. 'Besides, she's not really interested, are you, Nancy?'

Nancy smiled. 'Not really.'

'Kate will tell you all about it anyhow,' said Simon.

The following morning Caterina collected Kate as she had promised and drove her to a large clearing where trestle tables were being laid and decorated with exotic fragrant flowers by women and girls in their gay *pareus* with flowers tucked behind their ears and their laughter filling the air.

Caterina showed Kate the deep pits which would be filled with wood and volcanic stone and then after they had burned and the fire died down, the stones would be glowing with heat and the sucking pigs would be put on them. Banana fronds and wet banana leaves and finally wet copra sacks and then earth would be put on top of it all.

'It sounds an awful lot of work,' remarked Kate.

Caterina, trim in a linen suit of strawberry pink, a coolie-type straw hat on her ash-blonde hair, laughed.

'Just wait until you taste it, Kate, it's delicious.'

It was pleasant under the tall shady palm trees and Caterina led Kate to a long table where there were flowers being made into *leis*. There was every kind and colour of flower, each one as lovely, and Caterina explained what they were for.

'Each girl that comes to the feast has to choose a different flower, Kate. One flower is taken from each *lei* and laid on a tray made of plaited palm fronds and the tray is taken to Simon, whose eyes are blindfolded. He has to pick a flower at random and the girl whose *lei* contains the matching flowers is the Queen for the evening. Which flower will you have, Kate? This lime-green one is specially lovely, I think, don't you?'

Kate looked at the lily Caterina indicated. It was indeed exquisitely beautiful, not only the colour but the shape of the petals.

'Yes, it's very lovely,' Kate agreed.

'Then that is your choice, Kate,' said Caterina with a smile. 'I think this rose-coloured flower for Nancy, do you?'

'Yes, it's also lovely, but which will you have?' Kate asked.

Caterina looked thoughtfully at the flowers on the table and then picked up a small round white flower.

'I like this one . . . I shall be but a moment, Kate,' she added, turning to a big stout woman in a bright red *pareu* with a striped lily behind one ear. Caterina spoke softly and Kate could not understand what they were saying, only that the big stout Polynesian woman was arguing about something and when Caterina obviously insisted, the Polynesian woman threw up her hands in the air as if she knew it was hopeless to go on arguing.

Caterina turned to Kate and led her back to the car.

'Wear your prettiest frock tonight, Kate,' Caterina told her. 'It is an important occasion in the lives of the islanders.'

'But Simon said they're always having feasts.'

Caterina laughed. 'So they are, but each one has its own importance. They are eager to pay Simon compliments, for they see him as the only man who can save them from starvation and eventually emigration from their beloved island. Once upon a time they made good livings from copra, but the trade is dying away now and the hurricanes have done much to destroy their crops. Simon is

171

giving new life to the island,' she finished.

Caterina dropped Kate at the big house and then sped down the road towards the hospital. Kate walked to Adam's office and he looked up with a smile.

'Interesting?'

Kate nodded. 'They go to a terrible lot of trouble.'

'It isn't trouble to them,' Adam pointed out. 'They love it. You'll enjoy tonight, Kate.'

'So everyone says,' Kate replied. She opened the ledger she was working on and a companionable silence filled the hut.

That evening Kate looked in her wardrobe for her prettiest frock. She had to have something to set off the lime-green lilies that would be the flowers of her *lei.* Finally she picked an oyster-white satin frock. Miss Stern had chosen it, though Kate had said it was too expensive and that she would have no occasion for which it would be suitable. It was a straight frock with deep pleats either side. She shampooed her hair and set it so that it was a long straight bob with curled ends.

She went downstairs and found the rest of them waiting for her. Nancy had chosen a pale blue frock. Simon was immaculate in a white dinner jacket and black trousers. Jerome wore evening clothes, also, but

Adam was in a dark suit.

Taro drove them to the feast. He was dressed in his best suit, and he sang as he drove them. Already a great moon was climbing up the dark sky and the sound of music drifted on the soft wind.

The clearing was brilliantly lighted by great torches on stands and the whole of the island seemed to be there. Pretty Polynesian girls met them as they got out of the car and put wreaths of sweet-scented *tiare* flowers round their necks. The *papae,* or white people, were given chairs on which to sit, but the Polynesians all preferred the ground.

The tables were weighed down with food — all kinds of fruit and fish as well as roast pig.

Caterina, on Simon's right, for Simon sat in the place of honour as the guest of the evening, glanced across the table at Kate with a smile.

'Was I right? It was worth the trouble?'

Kate smiled. 'You were right, Caterina.'

'As usual,' Simon joked. 'That's the irritating part about you, Caterina. You are always right.'

'You admit that?' Caterina said, but the laughter in her voice had gone and her dark violet eyes seemed to smoulder as she looked at him. 'And yet you still . . .'

Simon put his hand on hers. 'Please, Caterina, not tonight,' he said, and there was a stern note in his voice.

She turned away, shrugging her shoulders slightly, and turned to Jerome who was on her other side.

After they had eaten and drunk various strange-tasting drinks, a tall dignified Polynesian rose and made a speech in pedantic yet poetic English as he thanked Simon for all he was doing.

'While we rested in the strong wise arms of your great-aunt, we were happy, and we wept when she left us and we could only sing for joy when you came to take her place. Here is one who loves us, we said gladly, for we had been through a time of great puzzlement but once again, the sun shone . . .'

Simon stood up to answer. He looked so virile and strong, so reliable, Kate thought. No wonder the islanders respected him.

Simon's speech was short, but worded in the same poetic way. 'I find it very good to be here with you. I am still young and foolish and have much to learn before I am wise like my great-aunt. This is a difficult time, but we have no need to fear the future. We will work as a family and make this island happy and prosperous again.'

He sat down amidst cheers and clapping, and Kate felt the same goose-pimples on her skin that she had felt when Simon had recited the poem about the rainbow shell. His deep voice was very moving, his whole attitude towards the islanders was so sincere.

There was dancing to follow and the guitars played the tantalizing, intoxicating music of the Polynesians as the girls danced, their long grass skirts whirling, their shapely arms moving to the rhythm, their bodies twisting and moving. Men joined in some of the dances, twirling and twisting.

Then the dignified Polynesian rose, clapped his hands and the music stopped at once.

Simon was led forward into the centre of the clearing as the dancers made a great circle round him. With much laughter and clapping, a very pretty Polynesian girl tied a big white scarf round Simon's eyes. Immediately several Polynesian girls came round with trays of *leis* of flowers. Apparently each *lei* was marked with the name of the girl who had chosen that particular flower, for immediately one girl came to Kate and put the lime-green lilies round Kate's neck.

The musicians began to play a haunting tune with a strange beat to it, and when the *leis* had all been distributed, one girl took a large tray covered with flowers forward and stood before Simon, saying something to him.

Kate, standing next to Caterina and Nancy, shivered. It was a strange tense moment watching Simon put out his hand, let it rest for a moment above the tray, and then pick up a flower, holding it high in the air so that everyone could see it. Kate caught her breath with mixed dismay and delight. Simon was holding a lime-green lily in the air. Even as she saw this, she felt Caterina give her a gentle push forward so that Kate could be seen.

There was a strange silence from the onlookers and then a sudden chatter followed by laughter. The pretty Polynesian girl was untying the scarf round Simon's eyes and for a moment he stared at Kate without moving.

Then he walked forward, taking her hand in his, turning her round as he bowed to the crowd of on-lookers.

Someone shouted something — Kate could not understand what it was he said, but Simon smiled and bent down to kiss her on the cheek.

There were sudden shouts from the crowd, mixed with laughter. One sentence seemed to be repeated again and again.

'What are they saying, Simon?' Kate asked.

Simon looked at the slight girl with the young bewildered face, at her straight silky honey-brown hair, her slim body in the oyster-cream frock and the lime-green *lei* round her neck.

'They are saying it was not a proper kiss. That the queen of the evening deserves something better,' he told her.

He saw the swift fright in her eyes, but before she could speak, he put his arm round her, and with his other hand turned her face towards him. She felt breathless and startled, unprepared for his action and for the close way he held her. As his mouth came down on hers, firm and hard on her lips, she closed her eyes.

She did not know how long the kiss lasted — she was only conscious of the warmth of his arms round her, of the strength of the kiss and of the fact that her lips responded to his. It seemed a moment that lasted for ever and yet was, incongruously, over almost before it had begun, but when he released her and all the circle of people round them burst into laughter, Kate did not know where to look or what to do, for she could only think of one thing — that she loved Simon. And by the way she had responded to his kiss, she felt he must know it, too.

Before she had time to move, the music started and Simon swept her in his arms. Simon danced well, and normally Kate would have enjoyed every moment of it, but she was too startled and embarrassed to enjoy anything.

As the music stopped, Kate and Simon found themselves standing near Nancy and Adam. Simon took his arm from around Kate and smiled.

'Nancy's turn now — if she will do me the honour,' he teased.

Nancy moved forward with a laugh and Kate found herself standing next to Adam.

He was apologetic. 'I'm not a good dancer like Simon.'

Kate gazed at him and hardly saw him. 'It doesn't matter,' she murmured automatically, and went into his arms.

Adam was a clumsy dancer, but Kate hardly noticed. She kept saying the same words over and over again to herself — words that didn't make sense and yet made the greatest sense of all. 'I love Simon,' she kept saying again and again. And suddenly she wanted to run and lock herself in her dark bedroom and face up to facts. How could she have been so stupid? How could she have been so blind? She should have seen it coming and made some excuse to get away, to leave the island, and escape before she got too badly hurt.

For she knew that was all that could happen. Simon was in love with Caterina, Kate felt certain of that. Just as Jerome thought, too. And who could compete with Caterina? Kate thought miserably.

The music stopped and Jerome was there. 'May I, Kate?' he asked.

It was a relief to go into Jerome's arms. He was a deft, practised dancer and she could relax. She found herself fighting a desire to tell him, to weep on his shoulder, to have him comfort her, for somehow she must find a way to leave the island. She could not bear to go on living there, loving Simon and having to watch him loving Caterina.

'You look very lovely tonight, Kate,' Jerome said. She glanced at him, her cheeks hot. 'Thanks, Jerome.'

'Very lovely,' he said thoughtfully. 'D'you know something, Kate?' he asked. 'Tonight, for the first time, I saw you as a woman.'

The quick frightened colour flooded her cheeks. Had it been so obvious, she thought with dismay, her discovery that she loved Simon? Had her response to his kiss betrayed her to everyone?

'Why?' she asked Jerome, more to cover up her embarrassment than for any other reason.

He smiled at her. 'You have a youthful dignity which is enchanting. You behaved very well when the crowd told Simon to kiss you properly. You were not coy nor shy. I was proud of you, Kate.'

Kate's eyes smarted. 'Thanks, Jerome,' she said. 'I didn't have much choice.'

'Nor did Simon,' Jerome said wryly. 'He's the last man to force a kiss on a girl who is unwilling.'

'Did I look so unwilling?' asked Kate, startled.

Jerome smiled. 'Forget it, Kate, you behaved very well.'

Kate tried to smile. Was he comforting her? Had Simon realized . . . ?

It was a terrible evening for Kate. She could not plead a headache and escape as she would have liked, for being Queen of the evening, she was an important person and special dances were performed for her, and she had to sit by Simon and dance often with him. They spoke little, which helped Kate overcome her initial dismay, but she felt most absurdly weak every time he looked at her. It was as if his strange grey-gold eyes could see into her mind, read her every thought, and she wondered how she could ever bear it if he discovered that she had fallen in love with him.

The laughter and the loud music seemed to get noisier and noisier and once, dancing with Simon, Kate closed her eyes, trying to retreat from it all.

'Headache?' Simon asked.

Kate opened her eyes quickly and looked up at him. 'I'll be all right.'

'There's no need to suffer,' he said, his voice dry. 'They don't need us now.'

Before Kate could say anything, Simon had led her to the car and was driving her home. Kate relaxed, closing her eyes. Soon she would be alone, able to think this matter out sanely. Perhaps she had imagined it all — perhaps all girls responded to a kiss as she had done. It needn't necessarily mean love, need it? she asked herself.

But it was a waste of time, she knew that, trying to convince herself that she was not in love with Simon. Suddenly she realized that it was taking them a great deal longer to drive home than it had taken them to reach the feasting place. She opened her eyes and realized with a shock that Simon was not driving her home, for the car was climbing a narrow mountainous road, going higher and nearer towards the mountain peak.

She sat up. 'What . . .' she began.

Simon was relaxed behind the wheel. He did not bother to turn his head. 'I thought some fresh air would do you good.'

'But . . .'

She caught her breath and stopped speaking. What was the good of arguing with a man like Simon? He always got his own way. She sat very still as Simon drove off the main road and on to a flat plateau of rock. As he stopped the car, she gazed ahead, catching her breath again, but this time with delight.

Had she ever seen anything so beautiful as the moonlight on the water? They were high above the lagoon and could see far out into the dark ocean with the moon's wide swathe of silver.

Simon lit a cigarette and twisted in the car to look at her. 'What upset you, Kate?' he asked abruptly. 'Was it the kiss?'

She stared at him and could feel the blood draining from her face. So he knew! Knew that she had fallen in love with him!

'In a way . . .' she began.

'But, Kate,' he said, and now there was

amusement in his voice, 'what's in a kiss? Especially a kiss like that when we have an audience cheering us on.'

So he did not know she loved him, Kate realized with a shock of relief, followed the next moment by annoyance at his tone.

'A kiss should . . . a kiss is . . .' she began to try to explain. She stopped speaking because of the way Simon was staring at her.

Then he nodded. 'I agree that a kiss can be a very serious matter at certain times, but . . .' he frowned, 'you must have been kissed before?'

Kate coloured. 'Of course, but . . .'

She had been going to say 'but never like that.' However, Simon gave her no chance, for he interrupted her.

'But not often?' He lifted his hand as he saw she was about to speak. 'Please, Kate, not again! I know — you were far too busy looking after your family to have time for . . .'

Kate's anger flared up unexpectedly. 'I wish you'd stop sneering about it. I never minded looking after them . . .' she began.

His hand moved and closed over hers, holding it prisoner. Kate shivered. It was absurd, but it was like an electric shock — stirring her deeply.

'I'm not sneering at you, Kate,' he said gravely. 'I admire and respect you for what you did for them, but it's no longer necessary. It's time you lived your own life, otherwise Jerome will feel he's cheated you out of something.'

Kate was startled. 'But he hasn't!'

'Not yet, but you must lead your own life now, Kate,' Simon said sternly, his face in the moonlight looking grim and stubborn. 'It's time you grew up.'

Kate was silent. She had grown up. She knew that now. This was love — this feeling of weakness, this desire to have him touch her and yet at the same time, the feeling of fear in case he did so, because she wondered how she could hide her love for him. She stared ahead of her miserably. Why had it to happen to her like this? She knew that Simon had only to say the word and she would follow him round the world.

'Adam's a nice guy,' Simon said unexpectedly, starting the car. 'You get on well together.' He reversed the car on to the road and turned to look at her. 'You like him, don't you?'

Kate nodded silently. What was Simon suggesting?

'Well, that's something,' he said cheerfully.

They drove the rest of the way in silence.

Kate curled up in her corner, her eyes tightly closed. Was Simon trying to marry her off to Adam? Why? For her own happiness or because he thought it would be good for Adam to be married to someone quiet and sensible? If Simon only knew the truth, she thought miserably, and if only it was not the truth!

CHAPTER ELEVEN

The next day everything was back to normal, or so Kate kept telling herself as Simon took them down to the lagoon in the morning before the sun was too high and the heat unbearable. The gentlest of trade winds rustled through the palm trees as they reached the emerald-green lagoon.

Mike shouted to a small naked Polynesian boy who was standing patiently in the shallows, fishing spear in hand.

Mike looked up at Kate. 'I've been out with his big brother, Mopelia, in the outrigger canoe. He's promised to take me sailing.'

'Has he?' said Kate, looking down at Mike whose cheeks had browned from the sunshine and whose thin body had filled out since they came to the island.

How she had changed, she realized with a shock. A few months back, she would have been furious with Mike, for she had known nothing about his having gone out in an outrigger canoe! As for the thought of letting him go sailing — ! What had happened? Had her outlook broadened? Had she realized that once she had fussed unnecessarily? Or had she merely ceased to worry about her family? Had . . . something or someone taken its place in her heart?

She glanced at Simon who was teaching Nancy how to swim underwater. His lean virile form was brown from sunshine, his fair hair smooth from the water, his voice quiet as he talked to Nancy, who was listening impatiently.

Kate looked away quickly. It was better not to look at Simon — someone might see more in the look than Kate wanted seen. It was wiser to look up at the mountain peaks covered with palm trees, at the bushes and creepers with their huge creamy white and crimson flowers — wiser to look at the old Polynesian woman walking along the sand in a black Mother Hubbard dress, a relic of the early days of the missionaries, or to gaze admiringly at the girl by her side with long black hair and a creamy flower behind one ear as she seemed to float along, so gracefully did she move, in her crimson *pareu* and her dark eyes watching curiously as she passed the group of white people wearing

187

such queer headgear as they went into the water.

When it was Kate's turn to have a lesson, she felt clumsy and nervous, but Simon was as patient with her as he had been with Nancy, showing her how to adjust the face mask and flippers.

Once in the water, she was startled at how lightly she seemed to walk, her arms and legs moving like palm fronds in a gentle breeze. Suddenly Kate felt happy, her hand in Simon's, as they moved silently through the warm water, surrounded by the little fish, all so many bright colours. Simon pointed out a parrot fish and a tiny purple fish, he showed her the bright canyons of coral and the sea anemone's gently-moving petals. He showed her caverns with pillars of pink and white and purple alabaster, and emerald and sapphire-coloured fish, sea-urchins as big as footballs, and sea-horses as small as shrimps. It was a strangely unreal time for Kate, her hand in Simon's as they moved, partners in the wonderful new underwater world, but as they surfaced, the world of fantasy in which she had been so happy vanished.

'Your turn, Mike,' Simon called, turning away from Kate, showing plainly that the moments that had been so wonderful to her had meant nothing to him.

Kate and Adam walked back to the big house together, taking their time, walking in the shade. Nancy and Mike were untiring in their desire to master the intricacies of underwater swimming and persuaded Simon to stay on.

'Quite a feast last night,' commented Adam as he and Kate strolled beneath the palm trees. 'It certainly had everyone talking,' he added casually.

Kate stiffened. She made herself walk on, looking straight ahead, for she was afraid of what Adam might see in her eyes.

'How d'you mean?' she asked, trying to keep her voice steady.

'Well, in the first place Simon's surprised look when he found he'd chosen you as the Queen of the evening,' Adam went on, holding back a low branch for Kate to walk on the path. 'What made you choose the lime-green lily, Kate?' he added casually.

'I don't know,' said Kate, trying to remember. 'It was a very pretty colour.'

'And had a delicious scent. Did you notice that?' Adam asked.

Kate nodded. 'Now you mention it, I did, but I didn't think anything of it at the time. Why?'

Adam chuckled. 'I just wondered. You see,

that lime-green lily is always worn by Caterina.'

'Caterina?' Kate echoed, her body suddenly tense as she remembered that it had been Caterina who pointed out the lime-green lily, Caterina who had said that Kate must choose that one as she thought it so beautiful.

'Yes. Simon knows that scent and always chooses that flower. It's quite a joke on the island, because they see it as a sign that one day Caterina will be the Queen of the island, just as Simon is the King.'

'Everyone thinks they'll marry?' Kate said, her voice light.

'It's obvious, isn't it?' said Adam. 'Didn't Caterina tell you when you chose the lily that it was her usual choice?'

Kate shook her head. 'No. Perhaps . . . perhaps as I'd chosen it, she didn't like to . . . ? She hastened her steps, glad to see the big house so close. 'Adam,' she turned to him, 'I've got an awful headache.'

'I am sorry,' he said at once. 'You'd better go and lie down, then. If you're no better later, Tehutu can bring up your lunch.'

'I think I'd like that,' Kate said, and smiled, conscious that it was an unsteady smile, as she hurried to the big house, up the stairs and into the blessed quiet of her bedroom. Here she could lock the door and fling herself face down on the bed.

Caterina had planned it all — to punish Simon. It had been Caterina who had said Kate must wear the lime-green lily — Caterina who had suggested it in the first place — Caterina who had pushed her forward when Simon chose the lime-green lily. No wonder Simon had been surprised when the sash that had blindfolded him was removed and he had seen Kate standing there.

But then, Kate realized, Simon had taken his revenge. That must be why he had kissed her passionately, had held her so tightly — because he had wanted his revenge on Caterina for the trick she had played on him.

Why, oh, why, Kate asked herself, had they to hurt her in order to hurt each other? Why use her as a weapon? But it was too late to ask questions that could never be answered, for the damage was done. The kiss had awakened her, had made her understand many things for the first time, for now she knew what it meant to be in love.

A gentle knock came on the door and Jerome called:

'Are you all right, Kate?'

Kate sat up quickly. 'Just a bad headache, Jerome. I'll be all right!' she called back.

'Like us to send up your lunch?' he asked.

'Please,' she said, her voice slightly unsteady.

'Kate, is . . . is something wrong?' Jerome
sounded anxious.

'Nothing at all . . . honestly,' Kate told
him, feeling instantly guilty, for she knew
how important it was to Jerome that they
should all be happy. 'I think maybe the
sun . . . or the drinks last night. I'll be all
right this afternoon, Jerome. Really I will,'
she called to him.

'All right, then. See you later,' he said.

Kate stood up and straightened her
crumpled frock.

She went to the wash-basin and bathed
her face in cold water. Then she drew the
curtains to shut out the blinding sunlight,
unlocked her door, and lay down with her
eyes closed.

This was something to be faced. She could
not just walk off the island and out of their
lives. Jerome would be terribly hurt and
would blame himself for having brought
them there in the first place. She must find
a way to live with this . . .

She must have slept, for when she awoke,
Tehutu was by her side, the tray in her
hand, a deliciously light cheese soufflé on a
plate.

Kate was surprised to find she was hungry,

192

and after she had eaten, she showered and changed into a cyclamen pink cotton frock. Feeling somewhat guilty, she hurried downstairs, for there was so much work waiting to be done, but in the hall was a note for her from Adam.

'I hope your headache is better, Kate, but in case you feel energetic, forget it. The office is closed, as Nancy and I are being taken to see the building sites.'

Kate felt relieved. It would be easier to watch Caterina and Simon together if she had a few more hours first in which to get control of herself. On an impulse, she ran upstairs to fetch the studio key. Soon she was sitting in the annexe to it, curled up in a chair and reading one of the diaries.

Kate's own pain made her understand even more keenly the anguish Adèle Scott felt after her husband's death.

'There are times when I wonder why I go on living,' Kate read. 'My life no longer has any meaning. The loneliness is more than a human being can endure. Why did he die? Why am I alone? I ask myself a hundred times, nay, a thousand times a day. I hear the girls laughing and singing and I wonder if I shall ever smile again. One day, yesterday to be precise, I was feeling like that and I went for a walk. I found a narrow path that must have been trodden by Polynesian feet for more years than I shall ever know and I found this *marea* — the Polynesian word for temple. And then I saw a *tiki* — their word for god, and they have a great many gods. This *tiki,* however, was different. The *tikis* are carved out of great chunks of stone and are square and ugly and stern. This *tiki* smiled. Immediately I felt better. Now when I fight the tears I shall take a walk to the little waterfall by the frangipani tree and perhaps the *tiki's* smile will help me.'

Kate lowered the diary, closing it gently. Never had she heard of a smiling *tiki.* They were hideous, cruel-looking creatures. Perhaps Mrs. Scott's smiling *tiki* could help her?

Quickly locking the door of the studio, Kate went upstairs to put away the key and to change into some flat-heeled shoes. She put on a large shady pink hat that matched her frock, as she knew it would be hot in the sunshine.

It was very still in the big house as she left it and she thought the Polynesian girls were probably resting in their own quarters. Simon must have taken Nancy and Adam to the building sites, Kate decided, as she walked along the garden path, past the thatched summer house, the wide beds of tropical, scented flowers in their blazing colours of deepest crimson, flamboyant scarlet, bright yellow and a dark blue. Kate had a good idea where the temple must be, for the frangipani Mrs. Scott had mentioned was now an enormous tree and could be seen plainly from the garden and there was a tinkling waterfall nearby. She found the hard trodden path and was glad of the shade of the palm trees. Looking around, she thought how quiet and eerie it was. The overgrowth had been allowed to grow and sometimes it was difficult to make her way along the path. She remembered that Simon had told her that the Polynesians refused to go near these old temples as they were terrified of ghosts.

She found the tiny but deep stream that wound its way tortuously through the undergrowth after first falling steeply down the side of the mountain. The rich creamy-yellow, sweet-smelling flowers of the frangipani pulled the branches of the tree down towards the water.

The bushes were tall and thick, all covered and interlaced with vines, but finally Kate made out what must have been the walls of the temple. The air was hot and steamy and Kate's frock clung wetly to her body as the perspiration trickled down her red face before she found Mrs. Scott's smiling *tiki.* Even then he was covered by the clinging hungry stems of vines, and Kate tore and tore at the wiry tough tendrils helplessly, unseen thorns scratching her fingers.

It was absurd, Kate told herself, but suddenly this *tiki* had assumed an importance in her life out of all sensible proportion. She felt that if she could see this smiling *tiki,* she would know that, like Mrs. Scott, she would find a way to overcome her unhappiness and build a new happy life, as Mrs. Scott had done.

Frantically Kate tugged at the winding creepers, wishing she had a chopper or a knife to help her — she concentrated on the face of the tiki and finally, with a violent jerk, she uncovered the lower part of the face.

'Got it!' she cried triumphantly, as she saw the strong ugly features and knew Mrs. Scott had been right. There was a softening of the hard unrelenting mouth — a suggestion of tenderness.

In the same moment, she felt something run across her bare arm. She turned swiftly, her hand moving instinctively to brush off the insect, but it bit her before she saw the huge hideous creature, more like an octopus than a spider, with long hairy legs.

Even as the stinging pain shot up her arm, Kate shook it violently and the spider fell to the ground. Kate turned blindly to run away, fighting an absurd feeling that the spider would chase her.

Clasping her arm firmly, Kate hurried back to the big house, remembering that Simon had constantly warned Mike to watch out for the tarantula spiders, whose bite could be fatal.

At the time Kate had thought with surprise that it was unusual for Simon to fuss about such things, but Caterina had told her later that Simon was right and that the bites were very dangerous sometimes.

Now as Kate hurried through the hot moist air, she was breathless and it seemed twice as far as it had been before. Her arm was beginning to ache and throb. She told herself it was sheer imagination, but as she stumbled up the path to the big house, she felt a wave of nausea overwhelm her.

How quiet and empty the house was — in the hall, Kate's legs suddenly seemed to give way and she collapsed, accidentally knocking over a small table that fell with a clatter.

A door opened and Kate looked up — through blurred eyes, she saw Simon staring at her. In a moment he had covered the short distance, had bent down and lifted her in his arms.

'What's happened, Kate?' he asked.

Suddenly she wanted to cry. She felt so safe in his arms which held her close and protectively. His face was still blurred, but she managed to speak.

'. . . bitten . . . a spider . . .'

She was close to Simon's face and she saw it change instantly as he carried her swiftly into the drawing-room, laying her gently on one of the couches.

She felt forlorn when his arms left her — for a short moment she had felt so happy. A brief glimpse of the happiness which she knew would never be hers.

Simon was kneeling by her side, gently holding her arm which was already swollen. His face was thoughtful as he took a handkerchief from his pocket.

'Not to worry,' he said quietly, using Ian's language for once, his voice matter-of-fact. 'We have so many spiders on the island, most of them harmless. All the same, it's better to take precautions . . .'

As he hastily tied a tourniquet round her arm, Kate felt deliciously close to him. She felt the warm firm touch of his hands on her bare skin and she tensed her body, willing it not to betray by any movement the love that she felt for him.

Simon turned his head and she found his face very close to hers.

'You're so hot, Kate. Where did you go?'

'To the small waterfall . . . I was looking for *a tiki* that smiled . . .' Kate began.

She saw the quick frown on his face, felt his hand lightly resting on her forehead and she managed a smile.

'I'm not delirious Simon . . .' she began.

He stood up, his face grave. 'Lie still, Kate, there's more to this than just a tourniquet.'

He left the room, and she obeyed him, closing her eyes, feeling, despite the dull throbbing pain of her arm, absurdly happy. He was so . . .

Her thoughts stopped abruptly as she heard Simon return. She opened her eyes and saw that he was carrying a tray which he put on the floor by her side, kneeling again, taking her arm in his hands. He bathed the bite gently and all the area round it with a soft cloth dipped in some liquid.

'Just milk,' he said with a quick reassuring smile. 'It's got to be cleaned before the next step.'

He sat back on his heels when he had finished and looked at Kate directly. The blurred vision had gone and now she could see his lean face clearly, could even see her own reflection in his eyes. It was the strangest sensation. She felt that for the first time Simon was really seeing her — as a woman. She did not know what gave her the impression, but it was strong and vivid. In his strangely-fascinating eyes she saw recognition and something else. Something like tenderness, even affection. Perhaps . . .

His quiet firm voice broke the dream that she had allowed herself to play with for a moment.

'Kate, this next part isn't going to be pleasant,' Simon said. His hand closed tight and warm over hers. 'I'm going to hate doing it to you and you're going to hate every moment of it, but it's got to be done.'

He took his hand away — did something to the tourniquet, releasing it for a moment or two, then tightening it. He turned away, and when he lifted his hand, she saw that it held a small knife that smelled of some strong disinfectant.

Simon held her arm tightly, his fingers like a vice, digging into her flesh painfully.

'I'll be as quick as I can,' Simon promised, 'but it's going to hurt.'

How right he was, Kate thought, as she closed her eyes tightly, fighting the tears of pain, biting her lower lip painfully as she tried not to cry out. He worked swiftly, but it seemed like centuries to Kate, then the knife lifted and Simon's face went down to her arm, and she felt his hot hard lips over the bite, sucking fiercely. In the same moment she heard the click-clack of high heels on the polished floor and heard Caterina's voice.

'Well, what on earth are you up to?' Caterina asked.

Simon lifted his head and spat fiercely into a basin.

'I thought I was disturbing a romantic scene,' Caterina went on, her voice sarcastic. She paused as Simon looked up at her.

'Kate was bitten by a spider,' he said curtly. 'I don't know which.'

Caterina's face changed and despite the elegant green silk suit, she became at once the doctor, moving forward, pushing Simon out of the way.

'What did it look like, Kate?' she said sharply.

Kate, still weak from the pain, murmured, 'It was big and very hairy.'

'By the small waterfall,' Simon put in. 'You know where the old *marea* is. I keep meaning to get it cleared of overgrowth, but . . .'

Caterina was bending over Kate's arm, nodding her head thoughtfully, adjusting the tourniquet.

'Time you cleared that part and stopped thinking about it, Simon,' Caterina said with unusual tartness. 'Go and rinse out your mouth at once,' she added sharply. 'And bring the car round. Kate'll be better in hospital.' She picked up a bandage from the tray and tied up the small wound neatly.

Kate tried to sit up. 'Just a bite . . .'

Caterina's hand was firm as she pushed Kate back.

'You'll do what you're told and no nonsense about it,' she said, her voice irritable.

Kate obeyed, closing her eyes as the light was hurting her. Why was Caterina so angry with Simon?

In a few moments, Kate felt Simon lift her and carry her out into the hot sunshine. She kept her eyes closed and her body stiff, for there was no tenderness now in Simon's arms. He held her lightly, almost impersonally, as if he was carrying a parcel of rubbish. She was laid on the back seat of the car and the cooler air coming through the open window as the car raced along the roads was a slight help, but Kate felt too limp and exhausted to notice.

Soon she was in bed in the hospital, a friendly nurse undressing her, putting a dressing on her arm, removing the tourniquet, giving her an injection. And then Caterina was there, wearing her white coat, bending over Kate, taking her pulse, temperature, sounding her heart.

Caterina straightened, her face stern. 'It was stupid of you to go to that place alone, Kate. We've warned you so often.'

'I wanted to see a smiling *tiki*,' Kate began, and saw the same sceptical look on Caterina's face that Kate had seen on Simon. Feeling too exhausted to argue, she closed her eyes. 'I'm sorry,' she said simply.

She heard the door open and Simon's voice, so she kept her eyes tightly shut. She felt that in the state she was, if she saw Simon and Caterina smiling at one another lovingly, she would burst into tears.

'How is she?' Simon asked, his voice sharp.

'It is too soon yet to know,' Caterina replied, her voice cool and slightly contemptuous. 'There is no sign of paralysis, but . . . It was fortunate for Kate that you were in the house.'

'Even more fortunate that you were paying me a visit,' Simon said, and he, too, sounded annoyed.

'Only because you had invited me,' Caterina replied sharply. 'I understood we were to have a discussion on what you called mutually vital matters.'

Simon's voice was hard as he replied: 'They no longer seem so vital.'

'On the contrary,' Caterina told him, 'this little episode makes me think that they are even more vital.'

'Caterina,' Simon sounded momentarily weary, 'I'm not in the mood to fight. Let's leave it until another day.'

Caterina laughed as Kate lay very still, trying to keep her breathing even so that they would believe her to be asleep. She could not bear to open her eyes — to see the way they must be looking at one another.

Caterina's laugh was suddenly soft, amused, understanding and placating.

'All right, my poor Simon. You have had enough for one day, is that it? We will postpone our important and interesting talk yet another time . . .'

Caterina's voice faded away and Kate heard a door close. She opened her eyes and found herself alone in the lofty cool white room. She moved her arm gingerly. It felt stiff. She still felt nauseated, but a delicious sleepiness was creeping over her as she closed her eyes.

How long she slept, how many injections she had, Kate never knew. She lived in a vague sleepy world in which she opened her eyes and closed them again, drifting on clouds of complete indifference as to what was going on around her.

She was startled when one day she awoke and was told she had been in hospital for three days.

'But was I really ill?' she asked.

Caterina, sitting by her side, smiled. 'What do you mean by ill, Kate? Were you at death's door? No. But if we had done the wrong thing, you might have been. Unfortunately you were allergic to some of the drugs we gave you and matters were complicated. Your arm is sore?'

Kate gingerly moved the heavily bandaged arm. 'It is a bit.'

'I'm afraid it will be for a while, Kate. I had to operate.'

'I don't remember a thing,' Kate said slowly.

'You were the fortunate one. We were worried. However, Kate, your illness did me a favour. Something that Simon and I have been fighting about for months has now been decided.' Caterina laughed happily. 'So, although it sounds foolish, I must thank you for getting bitten by a spider. Now, I must leave you.'

'Simon must be mad with me,' said Kate.

Caterina laughed again. She seemed a different person, Kate thought. Happier, more relaxed, much friendlier.

'If Simon is mad with anyone,' she said, 'it is with me, for as usual, as he would say, I had my way. Sleep well. Later today, you can have visitors.'

Kate lay very still after Caterina had left her. Why had Caterina changed so much? Why did she seem so much more friendly? Caterina had said she had had her way. What did that mean? How sarcastically she had spoken when she found Simon on his knees by Kate's side, his mouth against her arm. What was it Caterina had said? It was something about disturbing a romantic scene. Could Caterina have been jealous?

Kate drew a long deep breath. If Caterina had been jealous, the jealousy had gone now. Caterina seemed assured, almost triumphant. Didn't that mean, then, that Jerome was probably right and the obstacle to Simon's marriage to Caterina was Caterina's refusal to stop being a doctor? It seemed logical, even more so now, for if Caterina had won, as she had said triumphantly, then Simon must have accepted the fact that he was going to have what Jerome called a part-time wife. That meant — could only mean — that Simon loved Caterina very much indeed, Kate thought unhappily. But then she had always known that — for she had never hoped, even for one brief moment, that Simon could ever fall in love with her.

CHAPTER TWELVE

When Simon visited Kate for the first time, she felt that he was ill at ease because he roamed restlessly round the small ward, hardly looking at her, as he tested the mosquito screens at the window and the springs of the bed.

'You're comfy?' he asked. 'D'you find it noisy here?'

Kate was startled by the questions. 'I've been asleep most of the time,' she told him. 'I did hear a baby crying this morning, but . . .'

'Of course you've been under pretty heavy sedation,' he said, standing by the bed, looking down at her thoughtfully. 'You really feel better? How's the arm? Pretty sore, I expect.'

'A little. I'm sorry, Simon,' Kate said quickly.

His thick tufted eyebrows drew closer together as he frowned. 'Whatever for?'

'Being such a nuisance,' she explained, colouring.

'Forget it,' he said curtly. 'You weren't to know you'd walk into a spider, but whatever made you go there in the first place?'

Kate told him about the passage in his great-aunt's diary.

'She said it was the first *tiki* she'd seen with a smile.'

'I've never seen one. They were stern gods,' said Simon.

'But this one did have a smile,' Kate persisted.

Simon looked sceptical.

'It did, really,' Kate repeated.

Simon was looking at his watch. 'Caterina said I wasn't to stay too long, so I'll be off. Do what she tells you and don't rush things, Kate,' he added curtly, and left the room.

How empty it seemed after he had gone, Kate thought. His personality seemed to fill the room, and now . . . But that, she told herself, was something she must learn to accept — for that was the way it would always be.

She was glad when Nancy noisily arrived, full of chatter, curling up on the foot of the bed until the nurse came in with a frown, to give her a chair and then straighten the bedclothes.

'Not to worry, Kate,' Nancy said cheerfully. 'About your work, I mean, for I'm helping Adam in the evenings.'

'But I'll be back soon, and . . .' Kate began. 'Evenings are for fun.'

'It is fun,' said Nancy, curling up in the chair and tossing off her shoes. 'I never knew figures could be fun, before. Adam and I enjoy it, I promise you. In any case, Jerome and Simon have been coming up to the hospital every night, and scrabble for two isn't so much fun. I suggested if I helped that it might stop there being a pile of work when you got back and Adam jumped at it.'

'He's very nice to work for, isn't he?' said Kate, stifling a sleepy yawn.

'He's nice altogether,' said Nancy, suddenly darting to the window. 'What a lovely moon. Adam's waiting for me in the car. I guess we'll go for a drive.' She swung round. 'He's much more — more human, these days, isn't he, Kate?'

Kate yawned. 'Who . . . ? Oh, Adam. Yes, but I think he always was, but he had a very sad thing happen, Nancy. The girl he was going to marry jilted him and then got killed with her husband a short while later. Apparently Adam went to bits and lost all ambition or desire to live.'

Nancy stared out of the window. 'He never told me that,' she said slowly.

'I don't suppose it's a thing he wants to talk about. Maybe he's beginning to get over it,' Kate suggested. 'That's why he seems more . . . what you call human. I've always liked him very much — he's the sort of person who never has moods and is easy to get on with.'

Nancy swung round to look at her. 'Yes, you always got on well with him, didn't you?' she said in a strange voice. 'Well, I'd better be off, Caterina said we mustn't tire you.'

'Thanks for coming, and give Adam my love,' said Kate, and gave another yawn. 'I've never felt so sleepy in my life before.'

Nancy stood still for a second before turning to the door. 'You always were the lucky one,' she said, and left the room.

Kate's sleepiness left her for a moment. Why had Nancy spoken like that — so bitterly? Almost as if she was jealous.

The nurse came in, bustling round with an injection and a warm drink. 'Now we're going to have a good night, aren't we dear?' she beamed as she settled Kate.

Kate yawned. 'I don't think anything could stop me,' she said.

But something did stop her. Simon. Every

time Kate seemed to be slipping into sleep she would find herself remembering something Simon had said — or from behind closed eyes she would see his long thin face with the absurdly square stubborn chin — or feel again the electric touch of his hand on hers — or worse still, the hard warmth of his mouth on her lips as he held her close and kissed her.

'What's in a kiss?' Simon had said or implied.

Everything, Kate thought unhappily. Just everything. If Caterina had not arranged it so that Kate became the Queen of the evening, Simon would never have kissed her and Kate would never have known she loved him.

Or would she have discovered it in any case, one day? Kate wondered. Had she known she loved him for a long time and just refused to recognize it? Even when she had disliked him most, she had always been very conscious of him, very aware of his good looks and personality, very impressed by him. Had that been love and had she tried to refuse to admit it?

At last she fell asleep, but it was a restless night, disturbed with dreams in which she either lay in Simon's arms or danced at his wedding to Caterina.

It seemed a long week to Kate, but Caterina would not let her go back to the big house until the swollen arm was its normal size, and even then, Kate was told she must rest every afternoon and have a regular check-up.

'Maybe it sounds absurd for a spider bite to cause so much trouble, Kate,' Caterina said in her new friendly manner, 'but believe me, there are so many kinds of spiders and we don't know enough about them to take risks. It is better to be too careful than not careful enough. Tell me, why did you go to the falls, that day?'

Kate repeated what she had already told Simon.

'His great-aunt was very unhappy one day when she found this *tiki* that smiled, and somehow it helped her.'

Caterina gave her a shrewd look. 'And you were feeling unhappy and decided to look for the *tiki*?'

Kate felt her cheeks burning. 'I'd had a headache and felt a walk might do me good.'

Caterina looked amused. 'In the hot afternoon air?'

'I always forget it's so hot,' Kate confessed.

Caterina nodded. 'Simon was the same, at first, until he adapted himself to this new way of life. Sometime, Kate, I would like to read those diaries. Who has the key of the studio, or is it no longer locked?'

'I have.' Kate smiled ruefully as she went on, 'when Simon gave it to me he warned me not to lose it, so I always keep it in my dressing-table drawer. Any time you want it, Caterina, I can let you have it.'

'Thank you.' Caterina stared at Kate thoughtfully. 'You're working on these diaries?'

'Simon asked me to do a synopsis of them so that he could ask a publisher friend if they would make a book.'

'You think it's a good idea?'

'I didn't at first, but I do now,' said Kate. 'I think they'd not only be interesting but — help other people who are . . . are unhappy.'

'You are unhappy?' Caterina leaned forward. 'You're not happy on the island, Kate, are you? I know Jerome is always afraid of that.'

'I'm happy,' Kate said quickly. 'I love it here.'

Caterina seemed to relax. 'I'm glad, for it often worries Jerome. He says you came against your better judgment.'

'But I was wrong,' Kate said earnestly. 'Very wrong, Caterina. Simon was right — this was a wonderful chance for us all and

I'm very glad we came.'

Caterina smiled. 'So am I. It has done Simon a great deal of good — and Adam, also.'

'Then I can go home tomorrow?' Kate asked.

Home! The big house is home to me, she thought, but it won't always be for in the end, we'll have to go and Caterina will live there with Simon, she knew.

Caterina stood up. 'Yes. I will arrange for Taro to fetch you, but remember, don't do too much at first.'

'I won't,' Kate promised.

The car came to fetch Kate, and when she was back at the big house, she thought it was going to be difficult to carry out Caterina's instructions, for when Kate strolled down to the office she found Adam absolutely snowed under with work.

'Nancy told me she was helping you,' said Kate, a little dismayed at the work awaiting her.

Adam gave his slow sweet smile. 'She thought she was, Kate, I hadn't the heart to tell her she hadn't a clue, so I finally gave her odd jobs that wouldn't mess up what you'd already done.'

'But . . .' Kate began.

Adam stood up and came to Kate's side.

'Look, Kate, Nancy wanted to help me and she tried very hard indeed. She's a sweet kid, Kate. I only wish she was a few years older or I was a few years younger.'

Kate stared at him in amazement, trying to grasp what Adam had just said.

'You mean you . . .'

He nodded, his grave face lighting up. 'Yes, I mean just that. I'm completely, utterly and hopelessly in love with Nancy,' he said with a rueful smile. 'I know it's ridiculous of me, but I can't help it. I even dared to fancy I had a chance with her, but then, quite suddenly, she changed.'

Kate held her breath for a second as she remembered Nancy's visit to the hospital.

'When was that?'

Adam sighed, running a hand over his dark hair. 'I don't know — about a week ago. Yes, I remember,' he said suddenly. 'I'd driven Nancy to the hospital and we planned a moonlight drive, but when she came out, she said she'd got a headache and I had to drive her home, and she's been funny ever since.'

Kate sat down on the edge of a desk. 'Oh, Adam, how stupid can I be!' she said slowly. 'I remember that evening. It was when I was most frightfully sleepy and not quite all there, I think. I remember Nancy telling me how she enjoyed working with you, what fun you were and . . . and all that, and I said I'd always got on well with you and I sent you my love.' Kate's cheeks were hot as she gazed up at him. 'You know how one says that, without really meaning it. I mean, it's just an expression. Then — then she said something I've never forgotten. It was so unlike Nancy, Adam. She sounded bitter and jealous and she told me I always was the lucky one.'

For a moment they stared at one another silently and then Kate stood up. 'Oh, Adam, I'm so happy for you both. I'm sure she was trying to tell me she was falling in love with you and I had to go and spoil things. I'm so sorry, Adam. I'm sure if you tell Nancy you love her . . .'

Adam's eyes were bright with excitement. 'Thanks, Kate. I can't believe it, though . . . and yet in a way, I can. We were so happy together until . . .'

'Until I was so stupid,' Kate finished, moving impulsively to Adam's side and lifting her face to kiss him quickly. 'I'm so happy!'

A little cough made Kate swing round, startled. Simon stood in the doorway watching them.

'So you're back again, Kate,' he said slowly. 'Rather soon to be back at work, I feel, if this can, of course, be called work.' His voice was cool and faintly sarcastic and Kate knew that the fact that she was kissing Adam meant nothing to him. Simon turned to Adam, his voice impersonal. 'Have you those figures ready yet?'

Adam smiled happily. 'Yes, I finished them this morning. Here they are.' He held out a sheaf of papers which Simon took.

Simon looked at Kate for a second. 'No work today, Kate, and Caterina said a rest every afternoon. Remember?'

She nodded. 'I just wanted to see Adam.'

'There's no need to tell me that,' Simon replied, with the same cool sarcastic tone he had used before. 'It's obvious.'

After Simon had gone, Adam asked Kate eagerly if she really thought Nancy loved him.

'I can be patient. She's very young and I'm . . . well, I'm . . .'

'An old and senile man,' Kate said, laughing lightly. 'Oh, Adam, how could I have been so blind? She always liked you and I can even remember once that she said something about spending so much time with Ian, only because there was no one else who liked her.'

'I always loved her, I think,' Adam said

thoughtfully, 'but I felt she liked younger people.'

Kate's hand flew to her mouth with a childish gesture of dismay. 'I think I said that, too, Adam. I'm so sorry!'

Adam gave her a brotherly hug. 'Forget it, Kate. We all say wrong things sometimes. Now you'd better stroll back and rest or Simon will tear a strip off you. He's not in a good mood at the moment.'

'Why ever not?' Kate asked. 'I'd have thought . . .' She stopped herself just in time from saying something that was mere conjecture and not fact at all. ' 'Bye for now, and good luck with Nancy,' she added.

Adam smiled and lifted a hand and Kate walked slowly back to the big house.

It seemed strange to Kate that evening to be back again. Although she had not been in hospital very long, it seemed to have been long enough to make her more on the outside of the circle than ever. Simon was friendly in a formal manner, rather inclined to stress Kate's need for not doing too much too soon. Caterina, who had been expected to join them for dinner, was unable to do so, as there had been two nasty accidents at the building headquarters, and she was caught up in emergency operations.

Kate looked down the dining table and

saw the subdued excitement on Adam's face. His eyes were glowing and he was making jokes which Nancy did not seem to appreciate, her young, pretty face almost sullen as she ate silently. Once Adam looked across the table at Kate and smiled at her — and Kate noticed that Nancy had chosen that moment to glance up, had seen the smile and hastily lowered her eyes, but not quickly enough to hide the pain in them.

Kate enjoyed the exquisitely cooked dinner of crab soufflé followed by paw-paw and ice cream with grenadillas, and longed to be able to tell Nancy that there was no need to look so miserable, that happiness was just round the corner, but she knew that she must leave it to Adam; she could see that he could hardly wait to get Nancy off on her own.

But after dinner, Nancy seemed uncooperative, for when Adam suggested she teach him table tennis, she said she was tired. Jerome and Simon were talking and when no one was looking, Kate quietly slipped away. Soon Simon would take Jerome to his study and Nancy and Adam would be alone.

In her bedroom, Kate went out on to the balcony. It was a perfect night, the moonlight giving a strange new beauty to the palm trees, so still and dignified. She could see fishermen out on the lagoon in their small boats. Mike was sound asleep, she had slipped in to make sure. How well he was looking, and how happy.

Kate thought back over the months. How she had feared and hated coming here, how certain she had been that it was a mistake, and how wrong she had been. Nancy had met Adam, and what a wonderful husband he was going to make; Mike was a sturdy boy now, able to make friends with other boys, learning to enjoy studying; Jerome had a great future before him now that his work here was being recognized the world over — for visitors had come from the United States as well as Great Britain to see the new hotels that were being built and Jerome had been highly praised.

Kate went back into her bedroom and slowly undressed. It was early yet, but she felt absurdly weak and tired. She knew that she was postponing the moment when she must think of what had happened to her as a result of coming to the island, but once in bed, the canopy of mosquito netting enclosing her in a world of her own, she found courage enough to admit the truth to herself. She had met Simon and even though she knew that he would never love her, that she would only know heartache from loving him, yet she knew that she was glad they had met. How amazing he was, she thought, her eyes tightly closed. So changeable, so inexplicable, sometimes so sarcastic, other times kind; sometimes formal to a point of stiffness, at others friendly. How fortunate Caterina was to be loved by such a man.

Kate rolled over suddenly, burying her face in the cool pillow. And how it hurt, she thought miserably. How terribly it hurt to love someone who does not know you exist!

CHAPTER THIRTEEN

It seemed strange to be back at work again, Kate thought, as she took her place at her desk in Adam's office, but it had one blessing, she added mentally; it would stop her from thinking about Simon.

Nothing but sorrow could come from thinking of him too much. Maybe it would be easier if she left the island and went back to England — yet could she bear to voluntarily walk out of his life, she asked herself, never to see him again? She gazed blindly at the ledgers before her, asking herself which was more painful — never to see Simon again, or to stay here and dance at his wedding to Caterina?

Adam swung round in his swivel chair. 'I tried to tell Nancy last night,' he said, his voice quiet and urgent.

Kate looked up. There had been no chance to talk privately before, that morning, as Simon had walked down to the office with her, once more warning her not to overwork the first day.

Kate's face was bright with sympathetic interest. 'And what did she say?'

Adam looked rueful. 'Refused to believe me . . . and then burst into tears and rushed off.' He paused. 'Now what is there funny in that?' he demanded as Kate smiled.

'Simply that if she didn't love you, she wouldn't have cried,' she explained. 'Don't you see, she wants to believe it, but daren't, in case you were joking and she'd be so terribly hurt.'

'Women are strange cattle . . .' Adam began.

'That may be, but is it necessary to discuss them in working hours?' Simon asked drily, standing in the open doorway.

Kate looked up, startled, her cheeks suddenly hot as she saw the way Simon was staring at her.

'I think you are a disturbing element in Adam's office, Kate,' Simon went on, his voice sarcastic. 'He does double the work when you're not here . . . Adam,' his voice was curt now, 'I want you to get out the figures that Early Brothers sent us about five months ago.'

Kate was at the filing cabinet. 'I know where they are . . .'

'Thank you,' Simon said with studied politeness. 'Quite the efficient secretary. Adam and I are both fortunate in our staff,' he added, and left the coconut-log hut.

Adam and Kate worked in silence, watching Simon walk through hot sunshine towards the big house.

'What's the matter with him these days?' Adam asked. 'He never used to be so sarcastic.'

Kate shrugged. 'Love, I suppose.'

'Love?' Adam shrugged.

Kate wished she had said nothing. But Adam was staring at her oddly.

'Jerome and I think he's in love with Caterina,' she said finally.

'Everyone has been thinking that for months, but nothing happens.' He gave a happy contented laugh.

'You honestly think Nancy likes me, Kate? I mean, you think I should press on?'

'Regardless!' Kate finished for him with a laugh. 'I most certainly do, Adam. Try the strong man stuff, sweep her into your arms. It never fails.'

Adam looked at her oddly. 'You don't think she'd get mad?'

Kate laughed. 'She might pretend to, but I think she'd love it. Now, we really must do some work or Simon will sack me!'

'That'll be the day,' Adam said cheerfully, and bent over his work, whistling merrily if untunefully.

Tehutu brought them lunch on a large tray. Her pretty face was troubled.

'Doctor had to come for Meira, the gardener, cut his foot with an axe,' she told them. 'Blood everywhere!' She moved her hands expressively as she spoke.

'Is he all right?' Kate asked.

Tehutu smiled. 'He is fine. Everyone is fine when the doctor comes,' she said, and turned away to walk back with her graceful floating movement to the big house.

'Everyone loves the doctor,' Kate said, and was ashamed to hear the note of bitterness in her voice.

If Adam noticed, he gave no sign. 'Yes, we're certainly lucky to have her here,' he said cheerfully.

They dozed in their hammocks during their siesta and then returned to the office.

'You're not supposed to work in the afternoon,' Adam pointed out.

'I've just had a sleep,' Kate protested. 'I just want to finish this job, Adam, I'm bang in the middle of it.'

Adam hesitated. 'But . . .'

'Adam, stop fussing,' snapped Kate, suddenly cross. 'I'm not a child and it's all

226

ridiculous nonsense, all this fuss about a spider's bite. I'll just finish this and then go up.'

He looked at her stubborn back as she bent over the figures and gave a little shrug. Women! And then he thought of Nancy and began to plan what he would do that evening to make her listen to him.

Kate was startled as she walked back to the big house, choosing the shady paths, to realize how exhausted she felt. It was absurd — a few days in bed — a spider's bite, yet she had to force her legs and feet to move, almost drag them along. She ached all over and wished she had done what Adam had told her and come straight back after the siesta. As she came in sight of the big colonial-type house, she stiffened and stopped dead.

Simon and Caterina were in the garden. Caterina's face was bright with laughter as she faced Simon. Suddenly his hands were on her shoulders and he bent and kissed her . . .

Kate turned abruptly and walked into the glade of trees. Her eyes stung, her mouth was dry, she was stumbling over each small grassy mound or stone. At last she stood still, knowing it was madness to panic like this, for she could easily get lost. She straightened her yellow frock, patted her hair with her hands, tried to compose her face, and walked back to the big house. As she reached the door, Simon and Caterina, now sitting in chairs under a huge shady tree, saw her.

'Kate!' Simon shouted. 'Let me have the studio key, please!'

Kate nodded and then Caterina stood up, calling out something. Kate could not hear what she said, nor could she bear to linger, for Caterina's face was radiant with happiness and Kate felt that it was almost more than she could bear. Perhaps they had just arranged their wedding date — that would explain Caterina's radiance and Simon's cheerfulness. Why, he had not even commented on the fact that Kate should have been resting!

In her bedroom, Kate went straight to the dressing-table drawer for the key.

It was not there.

Kate's legs felt suddenly weak and she sat down on the edge of the bed.

The key must be there. It simply must be, Kate told herself firmly. No need to panic. She had always put the key there, so it simply had to be there. That was all there was to it — she must have imagined she could not feel the key there, for it had to be. It had never been kept in any other place.

She drew a long deep breath and tried again. The key was definitely not there. In despair, she pulled out the drawer and tipped its contents on to the bed. The key was not there.

Again she sat down, feeling absurdly tired. She had been so careful with the key, too, feeling it a kind of trust and flattered that Simon had given it to her. How could she go down and tell them she had lost it?

She shivered, imagining Simon's face, his annoyance, his sarcastic smile, probably some remark he would make that would hurt her terribly though he might not know it. And Caterina sitting there, so lovely and triumphant. How could she bear it?

There must be some way of finding it. Where could she have put it? She closed her eyes, trying to remember. As she had only returned from hospital the day before, then she must have used the key last on the day she was bitten by the spider.

She tried to retrace her steps that day. She had been reading the diaries and feeling miserable and had read the part where Mrs. Scott had found the smiling *tiki*. Kate could remember her own feelings at the time — maybe a smiling *tiki* could help her, she had thought. Now what had she done? Had she come upstairs after locking the door and put away the key? Or had she locked the door, popping the key into her pocket and gone straight out to find the *tiki?*

If only she could remember, she thought despairingly. Which dress had she been wearing? She went to the wardrobe and searched all her frocks, feeling in the pockets, but there was no key — and then she realized that, in any case, the frock she had been wearing on the day she was bitten would have been washed by now, and if there had been a key in the pocket, Tehutu would have found it and placed it on the dressing-table, just as she had done in the past when Kate had left a pencil or a letter in her pocket.

Kate glanced at her watch. It was late afternoon already — soon it would be dark, but somehow she must find the key, she told herself. The only alternative she could think of was that she must have dropped the key when she ran back after the spider had bitten her. She had kept to the path all the time, so the key must be close by it, if it had fallen out of her pocket.

She hurried down the back staircase and out of a side entrance which was not visible from outside the drawing-room where Simon and Caterina were sitting. As she passed the kitchen door, she saw Tehutu's startled face, but she hurried, not wishing to be delayed, as soon the short tropical twilight would fall and the night be there.

The trodden path seemed wider than Kate had remembered as she walked along it, bending down, glancing searchingly in the hope of finding the key. As she reached the clearing where the temple was, she straightened up and looked round her, seeing with surprise how changed it was. The loose vines that had clung so persistently to everything had been cut back so that the temple was plainly visible, and Kate turned round, looking for the smiling *tiki*. That, too, had been cleared of all creeping, clinging vegetation and stood alone, majestic, hideous and yet with that suggestion of a smile on its ugly mouth. The *tikis* were stern gods, Simon had said. But Mrs. Scott had been right, Kate thought; this one was smiling. She stepped backwards to get a better view and the ground seemed to give way beneath her feet. She screamed as she fell — landing on soft green rushes and creepers.

For a moment she lay very still, shocked and shaken. Gazing up, she could see the sky clearly. Gingerly she moved, testing her limbs. Luckily it was soft stuff she had fallen on, for no bones were broken. Slowly she stood and found that the top of the hole she had fallen in must be about fifteen feet above her. There was nothing on the stone-lined walls for her to use as foot-holds. She stood very still, trying not to be frightened, keeping her thoughts away from what might lie under the green stuff she stood on — spiders, scorpions, even snakes . . .

She gave a little gasp of fright she could not overcome and screamed.

It sounded faint even to her ears and she doubted its sound would carry above the hole. She pressed her hands against her mouth. Soon it would be dark. No one would miss her for hours. They would think she was dutifully resting until dinner time, and only then would they find she wasn't in her room. No one would think of looking for her here.

Something seemed to be crawling up her leg. She looked down, but nothing was there. Soon it would be dark in the hole and . . .

She pressed both her hands against her mouth and fought the panic that filled her. How furious Simon would be, for how stupid it had been of her to come here alone after what had happened before. She leant against the stone wall — had this been a well once? she wondered — trying not to cry, but the weakness and fear that filled her was too much and she could feel the tears sliding down her cheeks.

How long she stood there she had no idea. It might have been minutes, but it seemed like years, then suddenly she heard a voice . . .

It was the most beautiful sound she had ever heard in her life — Simon's voice.

'I'm here!' she screamed, but how faint it sounded. She shouted again and again.

'Kate!' Simon shouted, and his voice sounded closer.

It was quite a while before she saw his face as he knelt on the ground and looked down at her.

'Well now,' he said quite cheerfully, 'how did you get down there?' His voice was so matter-of-fact that some of the fear left her.

'Oh, Simon —' Kate gasped, choking on the words, half laughing, half crying. 'I was looking at the smiling *tiki* and . . .'

'Walked backwards and fell down,' he finished for her. 'My fault. I had to clear all this myself as no Polynesian would come near the place. I meant to have the well filled in later, but . . .'

'It's my fault,' Kate said unhappily. 'I shouldn't have come here again and . . .'

'Why did you?' he asked.

Somehow it was easier to confess the truth, now. Maybe because there was no Caterina looking on. 'I lost the key, Simon. I'm terribly sorry,' she said.

'But the key isn't lost. We thought you heard what Caterina called out. She borrowed the key this morning. She told me you told her she could have it and also where you kept it.'

Kate leant against the side of the well, her legs weak. Surely Caterina could have called louder — had it been a trick to frighten her and make her look a fool?

'Look, Kate,' Simon went on, 'it's getting dark so there isn't time to go and get help, but I'll soon have you out. I'm getting some vines and making a rope of them, so don't be scared and think I'm leaving you here.'

'Talk to me — Simon,' Kate called, suddenly fearful. 'I'll be all right if I hear your voice.'

'I'll sing to you if you like,' he said cheerfully, and sing he did.

Kate stood very still, trying not to think of the creepy frightening insects and reptiles that might be lying amongst the green climbers under her feet, and Simon's voice singing was close and then distant and then close again.

'I'm not as good as the islanders at this weaving,' he called down cheerfully. 'Luckily you're a light-weight.'

It seemed hours before he lowered a slender but tough rope of woven creeper to her.

'Now listen carefully, Kate,' he told her, his voice changing, becoming curt and authoritative. 'I'm tying one end to something firm up here and the end you have must be tied round your waist. I don't want you cut in half when I pull you up, so listen to my directions carefully and tie the knot as I tell you — repeat after me everything I say, so that I know you're doing it properly.'

She obeyed, repeating his instructions, tying the knot so that it could not tighten as her weight went against it.

'I'm ready!' she called. She was more than ready, she thought, fighting the hysteria that kept filling her as things seemed to be crawling on her legs and arms.

It was a bad few moments as he hauled her up — Kate vainly trying to get a grip on the smooth walls of the well, swinging with a frightening pendulum movement as Simon hauled her up — at last she felt his warm hands on her arms, hauling her up the last part and then holding her close. His arms were warm and strong and she closed her eyes as she rested her face against his damp shirt. She was trembling and she knew that if he had not been holding her, she must have collapsed on the ground. She had never felt so limp in her life.

She hated it when he took his arms away from her, but he kept one arm round her and led her to a stone bench. They sat down, Simon still supporting her. Suddenly she turned to him, burying her face in his shoulder and feeling the tears run.

She tried to stop, for Simon had told her once he hated women who wept, but it must have been the shock and fright and the effort of keeping from screaming so that now she felt as if she would never stop crying again.

'My poor Kate,' said Simon, and she was startled by the gentleness in his voice. He tried to dry her tears with his handkerchief as he went on: 'You've been unlucky ever since you came here. How you must hate the island. Did you know the six months are up, Kate? You've won our wager. You remember?'

Vaguely she knew that he was talking to her in order to give her a chance to gain control of herself, and the word 'wager' seemed to ring a bell in her mind.

'Our wager?' she echoed.

His arm tightened round her. 'Yes. I bet you that you'd all be happy on the island and I promised your favourite charity a thousand pounds if you were unhappy here.'

Kate's tears stopped as if a switch had been flicked off.

'But I'm not unhappy here,' she said.

In the dim light, Simon looked startled. 'You're not?'

Kate shook her head vigorously. 'I most certainly am not. Simon,' she went on earnestly, 'you were right and I was wrong. This is a wonderful place and we're all happy. I love it here — the beauty — the music — the . . . well, everything.'

'So I've won the wager after all,' he smiled.

'Yes . . .' Kate began, and stopped abruptly. Her mind was becoming more clear each moment. 'I have to pay a forfeit,' she said, her voice flat.

'Yes.' There was amusement in Simon's voice. 'And I'm going to collect it now. A kiss.'

Before Kate could speak, Simon had swung her round so that she lay across him and then he bent, mouth closing over hers. For a second her mouth responded, and then she knew that she mustn't let Simon know the truth. She forced her mouth to lie still and unresponsive, made her body stiff and unrelaxed.

In a moment he released her and helped her sit up. His voice was formal and unfriendly as he spoke. 'We'd better make our way back before it gets too dark,' he said stiffly.

Kate drew a deep breath. She felt chilly and forlorn without the protection of his arms.

'I hope you and Caterina will be very happy,' she said with equal stiffness, determined that he should never guess the truth and know that she loved him so much.

Simon swung round to look at her. 'We're always happy. We get on very well except when we're fighting.'

'Caterina told me that . . . and that she had just won,' said Kate, not sure why she was saying it, yet feeling she must make Simon think she was completely indifferent to him.

'Sure she won — and a long hard fight it was,' Simon said with a short laugh. 'I still wonder if I did right to give way. The new hospital will cost the earth.'

'New hospital?' Kate repeated, startled.

'Yes, that's what we're talking about, isn't it?' Simon asked. 'Both Caterina and Jerome want the hospital built before the hotels are finished. They say the accident percentage goes up each day — no matter what precautions we take, some happen. They want the hospital ready before the first guest arrives. I wanted to wait.' He gave a little laugh. 'They won!'

'But I thought . . .' Kate began, trying to realize what it all meant. The words came in a little rush. 'I thought you and Caterina were in love and . . .'

She was startled by Simon's reply. 'Oh, no, Kate. I admire and like Caterina, but she nags me too much. Besides,' he went on, 'didn't you know — surely you must be blind if you couldn't see that she's in love with Jerome.'

'Jerome?' Kate echoed. She turned eagerly. 'But that's wonderful, Simon, for he adores her. He thought, like I did, that you and she would . . .'

Simon shook his head. 'What a muddle! One thing, Adam and . . . he began, his voice stiff and formal.

'Nancy?' Kate said quickly. 'He's already proposed to her.'

'Nancy?' Simon sounded surprised. 'I always thought . . .' He paused.

'So that just leaves us, doesn't it?' said Simon, his voice dry.

There was a sudden stillness. Not a bird sang, not an animal rustled a leaf. Kate felt as if she and Simon were alone in the world — a tropical world with the sky growing darker every second and the sweet scent of the flowers filling the air.

'You were hurt badly once, weren't you?' she asked, the twilight perhaps giving her courage.

'Most people are,' Simon shrugged, his voice indifferent. 'Aren't they? I was very young, so it hurt. I thought the girl loved me and then I found it was my family's wealth she was interested in.'

'Simon, if you and Caterina aren't in love, why did she make me wear the lime-green lily?' Kate asked suddenly. 'She always wore it, didn't she, so that you could choose her? Then when you found it was me and that she had done it to hurt you, you took your revenge by kissing me.'

'Is that what you thought?' Simon asked, his voice strange.

'Yes.' So he wasn't denying it, Kate thought quickly. 'And if you're not in love with Caterina, why did you kiss her today.'

'You saw that?' he asked. 'We hoped you would.'

'You hoped . . . ?' Kate began, and stopped. Suddenly she felt unsure, afraid of saying the wrong thing.

'You won't believe this,' Simon went on,

his voice oddly strained. 'For you've made up your mind that I'm a hard, ruthless, sarcastic brute, but Caterina arranged the lily change-over in the hope of waking you up to the truth.'

'The truth?' Kate queried softly.

'Yes. You see, she knew how I hated the barrier you'd built up between us and she thought that when I kissed you, maybe you'd understand.'

Kate shivered. 'Understand?' she echoed.

'Yes.' He sounded impatient for a moment. 'Understand how much I loved you. Today Caterina saw you coming and suggested we kissed to try to make you jealous. It didn't work, though,' he added dully. 'Just now when I kissed you, I realized that I hadn't a hope — I knew that you could never love me.'

It couldn't be true, Kate was telling herself wildly. It couldn't possibly be true. Such wonderful things didn't happen in reality.

'But, Simon —' she began, 'that's why I went stiff. I thought you loved Caterina and I was afraid you'd find out that I loved you.'

In the stillness she heard him catch his breath and then, suddenly, she was in his arms. He was kissing her — her mouth, her cheek, her chin — and he was saying the most wonderful, most romantic, most sentimental, most lovely things to her. Words she would never have believed Simon capable of saying . . .

Suddenly he stood up, lifting her and holding her close. She slid her arms round his neck and gave him her mouth, lovingly, warmly, happily. He began to walk along the trodden path, pausing every now and then to kiss her again, as she lay in his arms and he carried her.

Once when he paused, he said softly: 'I have an idea that Great-Aunt Adèle would be pleased about this.'

Kate kissed him gently. 'I think so, too, Simon.' Suddenly she remembered something. 'How did you know where to find me?'

'When you didn't come back, we thought you might be resting, but Caterina went up to make sure, and you weren't there and your drawer was upside down on the bed, so she knew then that you hadn't heard about the key — when she shouted to you, I mean. Then Tehutu said she saw you coming this way, so I guessed you thought you'd dropped it and I came right away.'

Kate shivered. 'I'm so glad you came. I was scared!'

His arms tightened. 'You were brave. Very brave. Kate — when did you first know you loved me?'

Her cheek against his, she told him. 'When you chose the lime-green lily and kissed me. When did you first know?'

Simon chuckled softly. 'When I accused you of telling Georgia I had only given Jerome the job because I liked you. You were like a ball of fire, so angry with me. And you were right, too. I probably did create all the gossip by carrying you down the pier. Know something, Kate? I fell in love with you because you had the courage to defy me. I think I needed it.'

'If you knew how scared I was,' Kate confessed. 'Oh, we're home.'

The bright lights of the big house were in view. Her home, Kate thought happily, and then she glanced at Simon's face and she knew something.

'Wherever I am, when I'm with you, Simon,' she said softly, 'it'll be home.'

Somewhere in the distance, a girl was singing. A little sad but a romantic sound, a fitting background to a lover's kiss as Simon bent his head and Kate's arms tightened round his neck.

'Have I told you,' he said, 'that I love you?'

The employees of Thorndike Press hope you have enjoyed this Large Print book. All our Thorndike and Wheeler Large Print titles are designed for easy reading, and all our books are made to last. Other Thorndike Press Large Print books are available at your library, through selected bookstores, or directly from us.

For information about titles, please call:
(800) 223-1244

or visit our Web site at:
www.gale.com/thorndike
www.gale.com/wheeler

To share your comments, please write:
Publisher
Thorndike Press
295 Kennedy Memorial Drive
Waterville, ME 04901